I0666929

And just as you want men to do to you, you also do to them likewise. Luke 6:31

Be strong and of good courage, do not fear nor be afraid of them; for the Lord your God, He is the One who goes with you. He will not leave you nor forsake you. Deuteronomy 31:6

He said to them, "But now if you have a purse, take it, and also a bag; and if you don't have a sword, sell your cloak and buy one." Luke 22:36

Cover photo by Rosalyn Stowell
Photo of the author by Samantha Stowell
Technical Advisor: Mark Massingill

The Dark of Night
An Alaskan PAW Novel
Book 2

"I beheld the mountains and they trembled,
And all the hills moved back and forth.
I beheld, and indeed there was
No man.
And all the birds of the
Heavens had fled.
I beheld, and indeed the fruitful
Land was a "wilderness",
And all its cities were broken
Down
At the presence of the Lord,
By His fierce anger.
Jeremiah 4:24-26

Prologue

Just after I cross the last large bridge, my pickup has some steering problems and I almost go off the road. I slow way down and proceed with extreme caution. As I proceed, I see that several trees are down along the road that I didn't noticed before. These are close enough to come get for firewood. I turn my radio on, just to see if maybe that was another earthquake. All I find is static and dead air. That is not unusual with my radio and I think nothing of it until I get closer to home and as I start past Will and Shari's, I see them outside, sitting on the ground, holding each other. Something is wrong so I pull in.

Shari is crying and Will is upset. This does not look good. "Is it the baby?" I ask as I stop.

"No, Bubble Bump is fine. But I think the rest of the world is in trouble." she replies.

"The early reports are of massive damage and loss of life all over the world," Will says.

They have been using a broadband radio he bought a while back and are monitoring the short wave stations. None of the usual stations are on the air. He says the reports out of the Anchorage bowl area say there is no more Anchorage, no more Seattle and no more cities left standing around the world.

Major fires from ruptured pipelines. The underground facilities everyone thought were foolproof and completely safe have either collapsed or flooded out. Whole countries are no more. Islands have disappeared and a few new ones have emerged only they used to be inland mountains. There is speculation that possibly 2 or more of the countries developing nuclear weapons may have detonated at various places at about the same time and set off worldwide earthquakes of a magnitude beyond the Richter Scale.

We go inside their house and find only a few items out of place and it seems sound. I want to stop and check on Kara and Rose before going on home to see what damage my place may have sustained.

I pull into their driveway and see that Roman's cabin and buildings seem to be okay. I go on down the hill and the guest cabins seem to all still be standing. Kara's house looks okay from outside. I stop and go to the door. No one answers so I go on down to her Mom's. Kara is there and we go inside. Rose is fine and picking up a few items that had fell. Nothing major seems to have happened and the house looks okay. Kara says her place is fine, also. I tell them about thinking my pickup is breaking down. We laugh but it is not much of a laugh.

If Fairbanks didn't get hit very hard, soon there are going to be thousands of hungry people looking for food wherever and however they can find it. I tell them what I heard at Will and Shari's. There was no mention of damage to the Interior city or towns. We are far out of town, but not that far if they still have fuel to drive. All the military bases are a worry, also. That is a lot of people needing food in the immediate area.

Since it is late August, the nights are starting to get fairly dark again for a few hours. None of this is good news. I have to get home and see what damage I have and how my animals are doing. As I pull into my yard, I see a stranger sitting on my steps waiting for me. When he sees me, he places his hands on top his head in a classic prisoner pose. He holds this as I walk toward him with my handgun in my hand. "Who are you and why are you here?" I ask.

"My name is Jeremy Rhodes and I killed Rod and Rob before they could hurt Shari. I caught your goats after the quake and put them back in the pens. I've been keeping an eye on Will and Shari's place since Royal and his buddies showed up. I don't want to hurt any of you but I really, really need a meal and someplace to stay, if possible. I know you should just turn me in, but honestly, I won't hurt anyone here."

Strangely enough, I believed him. It had to be someone they knew, to get close enough to each guy and knife them while they waited in ambush for Will and Shari. I asked him exactly what happened that day, then said "Wait, why don't we go over and let you tell it to everyone here and we will decide what to do. After I check in the house first to see if everything is okay?"

He said he checked under the house and it looked solid and okay. So I unlocked the door and he went in ahead of me. There were some pictures off the walls and a few items fell from shelves in the living room, but overall, it looked pretty good.

We stopped at Rose's and she and the guys and Kara followed us over to Will and Shari's. Shari was shaken to see Jeremy but hugged him saying she knew he wouldn't hurt her. Seems he is her cousin.

Once we were all introduced, we waited for the story.
Jeremy started right from when they left the airport. He only came along to be the calm voice of reason, he thought, so the couple could talk over some legal matters needing cleared up by the death of Shari's folks. They did not think Rod was all that bad, and left him some property jointly with Shari, in their Wills with Rights of Survivorship. Rod decided he wanted it all. But Jeremy didn't know that until he was tied in the back of the SUV and heard what they were planning. He was to take the blame and they were going to use her own rifle to shoot her and if they had

a chance, Will, also. Rob was only backup and to make sure Will didn't show up too soon after Rod had his little talk with Shari. Jeremy finally managed to work loose from his bonds while they trashed the house. He went in as they were going out the back and they did not see him. He found the large sharp knife where they stuck it into a sofa back. He followed Rob first and came in behind him as he hid behind the old outhouse. He was making too much noise to hear Jeremy, who had been in Special Forces in the military, slip up behind him and slit his throat without a sound. He quickly stuffed him into the outhouse and then stalked Rod. He found Rod just as he was taking aim at Will. He wanted to taunt and punish Shari, so he was going to shoot Will right in front of her. The other woman (me) being there didn't even slow down his plans. He figured he would get to punish 2 women instead of just one. Jeremy slid silently up behind him and stuck the knife up under his ribs just as he started to squeeze the trigger and the rifle went off. There wasn't time to hide him or the rifle as we started directly for the sound of the shot. Jeremy just had time to get himself hidden before we got to the body. Then the Trooper showing up really made it impossible to do anything and Jeremy was afraid they would haul him in and he would never see the light of day again.

He had been keeping an eye on Royals' buddies since they were now wandering the woods out here, also. He apologized for stealing food once in a while, but eating berries and roots and small rodents just was not a good diet. He was sorry he took my cinnamon rolls in the greenhouse, but just could not resist. When was I going to make some more?

Well, since the earthquake, we had no idea whether or not there were any Troopers left to come out or if there were any type of Court system left in the State. We talked it over while Jeremy sat in the other room, and decided he probably had saved several lives by the 2 he had taken. If Will and Shari were willing to have him stay here, the rest of us had no problem with that. They were willing. He was very surprised when we told him the decision.

Then talk turned to the earthquakes and Will turned the shortwave radio back on for us to hear the updates. There were still a few HAM operators on the air and trying to let everyone know the extent of the damages. It sounded like the earth as we knew it was totally gone. There may still be a few small towns and villages here and there, but the roads, trains and shipping was gone. All the major cities? Also gone. It was hard to think that Fairbanks may be the largest city left on earth. It had no means of supporting itself, so it soon would cease to exist as a city, either.

I finally got home and unloaded my pickup. It would probably be the last load of anything I would ever be able to buy in town, ever. This was it, there won't be any more. Noah helped me put the feed away and unloaded the building supplies and rugs into the barn.

We are both silent as we part and he goes back to his camper which weathered the quake fairly well.

The next morning, we awaken to a freak snowstorm. There is about a foot of heavy wet snow on everything and more coming down. Oh, this isn't good for the survivors in town. If they have no electricity most won't have heat. As deep and heavy as the snow is, no one will be driving out this way, anyway, so maybe it is good news for us.

The snow continues all day and there is the crashing of tree limbs breaking from the load on limbs still covered in green and gold leaves. Trees are bending and the brush is almost flat on the snow banks. The wind has come up, so it is blowing drifts across the roadway, also.

I ask Noah if he wants to try making it over to be with his Dad and brother. He says no, he is comfortable where he is, but if it gets much colder, could he move into the little cabin out back? It does have a small wood stove in it. Well, yes, it would be nice to have him here.

The snow keeps falling and during the night, the temperature starts dropping. I feel sorry for anyone out in this weather and the poor folks without homes now are to be prayed for.

Early the next morning, I hear the sound of a snow machine coming in my driveway. It is the fellow we delivered firewood to, this summer. He comes to the door and says he is just checking to see if I am okay and is going over to check on Rose, Kara and the new folks. He asks about the earthquake so we tell him what we have heard on the radio at Will and Shari's. He is dumbfounded and just shakes his head. I ask him if he will be okay and he says yeah, he has over a years supply of gas for his snow machine and chainsaw and seldom ever went to town, anyway. I send him on his way with a bag of cinnamon rolls to either keep or share at each stop he is making this morning and invite him back for a meal on his way home. He accepts after thinking it over a second or two.

After he leaves, Noah comes to the door and I let him in. He has shoveled a path from the house to the barn and to the woodshed. I fix breakfast and he is very happy to come in and get warmed up and a hot meal. After breakfast, I start bread dough and a large pot of stew from the remnants of the garden.

I gear up and go out to care for the goats.

They are enjoying the snow. I think after a while they may get tired of it just like most humans do. At present, I am thinking it may be saving us from some unpleasant encounters with town folks. Maybe by the time they decide to head this way, they won't have fuel for the trip. Right now, the only way they could reach us is by snow machine and they would have to be hauling extra gas for the trip.

Late afternoon, the guy on the snow machine stops back by to let us know the latest news from the other direction. He found everyone warm and cozy and at Kara and Rose's they were even happier. Their kids in town had rounded up some motorcycles and trailers right after the earthquake, loaded up all they could find and came home. They got to the place just before the snow hit too hard. They said the bridge was out just north of town and they came through the river. The next bridge was cracked and they went over it one at a time, being very careful, the lightest loads first. Then at the last large bridge, they again crossed in the river as the bridge looked like it was not safe, to them. Town had been hit harder than the reports stated. The underground utilidor tunnels under the Bases and under downtown Fairbanks had all collapsed and no utilities were working. The runways were all buckled and broken. No flights could enter or leave, except helicopters and only if they had enough fuel in the tanks as the tank farm was on fire. The roads going south from Fairbanks were clogged with traffic thinking they could drive somewhere and get away from the disaster. No one was headed north but them.

Both of Rose's Great grandchildren made it out with their parent. Their community had increased, but Rose and Kara both planned on them being there in emergencies, anyway. Some of the little extra cabins were just for each adult to have their own place. The "adopted" ones were also welcome and also had been planned for. They hadn't exactly planned on the one grandson bringing both of his girlfriends out, though. That could get interesting in the days ahead.

We shared our meal with the man and he accepted another bag of rolls and some bread to take on his ride home. He left soon after and we were glad he had stopped by. That was the best load of firewood we ever delivered.

Noah and I sat and tried to figure out exactly what was going to happen next and how to deal with it. We know we could survive out here, if we are left alone. It sounds like Wasilla may now be ocean front property. So the coastline has changed drastically. I am wondering how Interior is going to change if the ocean levels are rising or have risen.   Most of the Yukon and Tanana valleys are not very much above sea level.   What if we now could catch ocean fish just down in our valley?   We will probably have to wait until the coming summer to find out about that.

4 months later:

Well, it is the end of the old year and what a year it has been.   The world has come to an end, as we knew it.   As far as I can tell, there will be no commerce or government as such, any time in the foreseeable future. Whatever supplies we have on hand in anything, is going to have to last, and last, and last.   There will be no running to the store if something runs out.   We are going to have to find alternatives for just about everything.   If not for ourselves, then for our children and grandchildren.

In some ways, the future looks grim, in others, maybe the best that could have happened to us.

There has been murder, there has been new lives enter our sphere.   There will be more in the future.   It is human nature.

I am going to get married sometime in the spring.   That is if we can wait until spring.

Chapter 1

New Year's Day dawns bright and sunny. No wind and only -10. We are slowly gaining sunlight each day and no matter what the circumstances, today is a lovely day. I am sure this winter is the last time we will be this secure and peaceful, but it is wonderful while it lasts.

I ask Noah if he would like to head over to check on the neighbors. He suggests we take the license Rose and I made up with us to see what we will need to do to get married. I mention the little detail that he hasn't formally asked and I haven't answered on that one yet. We smile at each other and get ready to go. He has healed up very quickly from his gunshot wound.

We are getting so used to the walk over to Rose's place that we are almost on the mound of something beside the trail near her driveway before we notice it. The dogs are curious but not growling, so it is probably not dangerous. As we move closer, we find it is the heavy winter coat Royal was wearing when he and Jeremy left a few days ago. Uh-oh, that does not look good.

Noah picks the coat up and adds it to his load as we turn in the driveway. We stop first at his Dad's cabin and visit a while with Roman and Thad. They have not seen either Royal or Jeremy.

We stop at Kara's next, and visit a while there. Roman and Thad have walked down with us. Then we all head down to see Rose. She is happy to see us but has no news about Royal and Jeremy.

We leave the coat. Someone may have use for it and since it was -40 when Royal and Jeremy left my place, he probably will not ever need it again. Then another thought flashes across my mind. We should have stripped the 2 men killed by the bear in my yard before burying them. Someone could have used those clothes, also.

We are going to have to really change the way we think, to make do when necessary. There really is never going to be any more items that we take for granted now, in any of our lifetimes. What we have now is probably all we are ever going to have. It is a very sobering thought.

Roman stays to talk to Rose and Thad drops off at Kara's. Noah and I smile about that and go on home.

By the next morning, the temperatures have dropped again, so it is another good day to work on the hides we are tanning. Before we start, we take care of the chores. Stoke the stove in the barn for the goats, feed and water them and take care of the chickens.

We are trying our hands at tanning the moose hide with the hair off, so that is a new experience for both of us. We have moose hair everywhere. I bag it up as we shave it off and think there should be a better way. I am also wondering what we can use moose hair for. Maybe make a mattress, or something. From now on, I am not throwing anything away, unless it is truly spoiled or ruined. I will save every scrap of paper to make rough new paper from, even. Everything is going to have a value.

The weather seems to be holding in the -30 to -40 range so we do a lot of work on the hides. The first day it is only -20, we hear someone coming in calling out to let us know.

It is Al, coming over for a fur sewing lesson. Noah is ready to quit on the tanning and this is a great excuse. Al has brought several furs he has tanned this winter, to learn on. He wants a hat, so we measure his head and lay out the pattern on the table. The furs he wants to use are dampened and stretched to dry, which doesn't take long and we have a small lunch while it is drying.

After lunch and the hide is dry, I draw the pattern on the skin side with some charcoal from the fire. I show him how to cut the hide only using a razor knife. If cut pressing down, it cuts through the fur also and ruins the piece.

He catches on right away and cuts out the rest of the pieces. He is using the leg pieces from old worn out blue jeans for the outside shell instead of leather. He is handy with a needle, so that part goes well. He is using beaver for the shell and marten to line it, it should be a very warm hat.

He finishes the outer part and only has the lining to make and decides he better go on home. He has the idea now on how it is done. We already have the liner cut out, so he only has to sew it together and then put it together with the ties.

As he is leaving, he pulls a beaver hide from his pack and hands it to me. It is a thank you for the help gesture. He apologizes for it not being tanned yet, he just hasn't had time.

Wow, I don't want to accept it, but he is adamant and I don't want to discourage him from coming back. So now I have a lovely beaver pelt to tan. Just before he leaves, he mentions he found a female husky along the road and wonders if he can bring her over to "visit" Pal later in the spring. He wants to get a team built up, so when he runs out of fuel for the snow machine, he will still be able to trap and travel. His other dog is neutered.

I think we are going to have to raise as many animals as possible for a few years to make sure we have stock.   I plan on letting most of my hens brood eggs as soon as they want to start.   The goats will be having as many as possible, I am thinking.   I will have to hurry up and read the books I borrowed from Rose.   I know they milk for 10 months after having a kid.   Gestation is about 5 months and best to wait until does are 7 months old or more.   Usually they have 1 or 2 kids a year.   This could take a long time to increase the herd.   I should have asked more questions when I bought these 2.

Winter is going by fast.   I have so many projects going there doesn't seem to be time to get it all done.   I know summer is going to be hectic as now a garden and greenhouse mean the difference in whether we will eat next year.   Then there is the hay cutting for the goats and gathering seed heads for the chickens. Firewood.   Nothing like a bit of pressure there.

Last summer seems like a relaxed walk in the park.   Just the projects I wanted to do and done at my own pace.

We work on finishing the upstairs of the barn when the weather is warm enough and stay working on the tanning and fur sewing, when it isn't.   We have a small trap line we are still running, but it is about time to pull the traps.   One of us checks it every other day.

My indoor garden on the sun porch is not looking very good, but it is still producing some fresh salads. The tomatoes finally all ripened and we now only have a couple of them left. The plants have been gone for ages, but the tomatoes stay in better condition left on the vines. Dead or alive.

The days are getting longer and by March 21st, we have 12 hours of sunlight a day. The snow has not even thought about melting. But we are enjoying the extended sunlight hours and decide to go see how Will and Shari are doing. The twins are around 5 months old now and probably a handful for Shari and Ashley.

We stop to see if anyone at Rose's place wants to go with us and Rose does. So we wait for her to get her gear on and then walk on over.

We brought some bread and some fur clothes we made for the twins. Will and Shari are happy to see us and when Ashley comes out of the back room with the twins, she is smiling, also. Jeremy comes in from the back door a while later and we all have a good visit. I want to ask what happened to Royal, but just can't bring myself to ask.

As we walk out the door to leave, Jeremy comes out after us. He wants to let us know Royal actually escaped on their way over here. He does not see how he could possible still be alive with his badly frostbitten face, lungs and hands, then running off without his coat. Jeremy grabbed his coat when he made a break for it and the coat pulled loose. Jeremy was trying to be kind by untying his hands so he could balance and maybe not freeze them worse than they already were.

He has been searching, without saying anything to the others, for Royals' remains. So far, he has not found any.

We walk Rose home and tell her what happened right after Christmas. She is amazed the guy survived to make it out here and what means of transportation did he use? I have been wondering about that myself.

When we get back to my place, we take care of the animals and I have a sneaking suspicion that we didn't separate the goats soon enough last fall. Nanny is definitely looking like we are about to increase our goat population. I think we better get a milking stand built soon and build a better pen to hold her and a possible young one or two. All I can hope is that the weather holds fairly warm and that she has no problems since I haven't a clue.

In the next couple of days, we reinforce the pens and build a milking stall. I have been grooming her and handling her a lot, so I hope she isn't like an ornery cow and puts up a battle being milked. We cut brush often to add to their diets, since we don't have a lot of commercial feed. I increase the amount of the clover hay I give her, slowly, so I don't upset her digestion.

When we go out a couple of weeks later, she has a very small kid at her side. Evidently she did okay by herself and it is a good thing. She was probably better off without us panicking. It is a darling little doe and I feel blessed that we now have 2 females. Now I have to learn to milk a goat.

That evening, I try my hand at it. We both are not sure what I think I am doing, but she is gentle and that is a plus. I don't want to separate her and her baby, but we won't get much milk if I don't. So I just milk out a little bit every night and every morning to get her used to it. I make some little fleece blankets to fasten on the little kid to help keep her from getting cold. I had no idea she would be so small.

I give the first few milkings to the chickens and they love the change of diet. Then I start saving it. I want to make some cheese so start digging through my cookbooks. Hmmm, maybe I will try making cottage cheese the way we did on the ranch when I was a kid. Then if that works, go on from there. I know the cream doesn't separate, so I don't know if I can make butter or not. I have heard of it, so it must be possible. I can see we may be feeding the chickens a lot of experiments.

I start a few garden seeds indoors but only a few just in case they don't make it on the sun porch. Then I cover some of the raised rows with plastic after sprinkling with ashes to speed thawing.   I will start a few more every week until I can plant outdoors.

We have pulled all the traps and snares as the furs won't be much good now until next winter.   I hang them up in the barn so they won't get odors from in the house on them and need cleaned again next season.

Al stops over to show me how he is doing on the fur sewing and he has done very well indeed.   He asks about what I am doing in the garden with the ashes and plastic, so I show him.   He has some old windows he thinks would work for something like that, and will do that when he gets home.   For a guy that doesn't want to be around people, he is a very good neighbor.

Chapter 2

I think we are getting it right on the goat milking and the kid is growing like a little weed. I take her blanket off during the day and only put it on her at night, now. She seems to be doing very well. Building her pen close to the stove probably helped, also.

The next time we walk over to see Rose, Noah asks her what we need to do to get married. She looks at me and I shrug. I love Noah and we are already living just next door so to speak. She tells him it only takes us agreeing and 2 witnesses to sign after the ceremony. It might be nice to make it a community event.

On our way home, Noah stops beside a nice small bench he built during the winter. He pulls a bag out from behind the bench and seats me on a soft cushion he places on it. Then he does the whole get down on one knee thing and asks me to marry him. Uh, if he had done this on the way over, we could be married already.

I say "Yes" and he sort of leaps onto the bench beside me and hugs me. Then he gives me a most marvelous kiss. Soft, lingering, yet very exciting. I think it is a very good thing we are outside in barely warm weather and snow all around. That was probably the most erotic kiss I ever had in my life. I'm thinking maybe we should walk right back to see Rose and ask her to set up a date and time and we will be there.

Noah pulls out another ring he has been working on at the cabin he stays in. It fits right around the one he made before that I have been wearing. It makes a most unusual design and I can see where a third ring will mesh into the design. This is truly a one of a kind ring and I will cherish it all my life.

Noah is late coming over for breakfast the next morning. When I go out to the barn, the chores are already done, so I feed and water the chickens and gather the eggs. A couple of the hens are starting to act a bit broody, so I place several eggs under them and let them set. These will be early chicks, but we need them. It is staying fairly warm in the coop, so they should do okay. It will be 21 days until they hatch, so I mark it on the perpetual calendar we made.

The days are finally getting above freezing, so we tapped several of the large birch trees to gather sap. It takes twice as much birch sap as maple sap to make a gallon of syrup. But it's not like we have other places to be and things to do. We have a small shed built away from the rest of the buildings to boil off the sap. Noah comes up the hill packing two 5 gallon buckets of sap, so I get the fire started in the barrel stove we are using to boil sap on. I have some old flat hotel stainless steel pans so they should work well to boil the sap in. By the time Noah makes it to the shed, he is thinking his arms have stretched enough to scratch his ankles without bending over. He will definitely only carry one bucket next trip.

We dump the buckets into the pans on the stove and he takes one back to finish the rounds of the trees we tapped. The season is very short for good sap, so we have to keep at it. As soon as the sap turns cloudy, it is bitter and done for making syrup.

It's a good thing we have a lot of firewood on hand. This sap boiling takes a lot of it. I'm glad we are outdoors to do it. Between the sweet odor and the moisture billowing out, inside the house would be unbearable.

Once some of the sap is evaporated down enough to consider it syrup, I take some in the house and use a candy thermometer to continue cooking until it reaches 300 degrees. I add a teaspoon of soda and stir, then pour the foam out onto a buttered half sheet pan. Tipping the pan a bit back and forth evens it out and I leave it to cool.

The rest, we make into syrup and bottle in canning jars. This may be the only sweetener we have after we run out of sugar. I will have to experiment on cooking with it, while I still have sugar to use.

The sap is a very refreshing drink, right out

of the tree, so I can several bottles of just plain sap to see how they do later in the year. We have just over a week of intense syrup making then the nights stay above freezing and the sap turns cloudy and we are done for this year.

The first garden rows are planted under plastic to protect them and I have almost everything started in the house now, to plant in the greenhouse later.

I think we are all caught up on what needs done that we can do at present. The ground is still fairly frozen in most areas with quite a bit of snow still around. No mud yet or bugs. So we decide to go visiting.

We are training the dogs to carry packs now, so we load up, us and the dogs, and head over to see Rose and Kara and the group living there.

As we near their place, we hear something no one has heard in several months. An airplane is coming from the north and it sounds like he wants to land on the straight stretch of road we are coming to. We hold the dogs and he sets down on the roadway. We walk over as he is climbing out of the cockpit. He wants to know immediately why the road isn't plowed this winter and no radio signals from Fairbanks. He just spent the winter up on the Porcupine, trapping and never saw or heard anyone all winter as his radio seemed to have quit working.

So we have to tell him what has happened and there probably isn't any Fairbanks to shop in or sell his plane load of furs to. He sits back down on the ground and just sits there a while. Then he walks on down to see Rose and consider what he is going to do next.

He has a nice cabin, a fair garden area and plenty of wild game in the area he lives in during the winter and usually does raise a garden there in summer also. He only comes to town often enough to resupply and sell furs. He thinks he has enough fuel to get home on if he doesn't hit any headwinds. He is not even going to go see what town looks like or he would not make it home for sure. With no source of fuel, this may be his last flight, ever. He does have some stored at home, but not a lot. He figures that will go for chainsaw cutting firewood until it runs out.

We wish him luck, help turn his plane around on the road and he takes off, heading north.

When we go back down and talk to Rose, we ask about getting married and when would be the best time to hold the ceremony. She is willing to do it at any time. We set it up for a couple of days later and go on home.

I start housecleaning big time. It's not like the house is a wreck or anything, but after a winter of shaving moose hide and tanning furs, it could use some airing out. It's not that I am nervous about getting married. But I am. The best thing to do when I am nervous is keep busy.

As I am getting ready to leave on the day we picked for our wedding, I hear people coming in the driveway. Everyone has decided to surprise us and come here for the ceremony. Well. I am certainly glad I was nervous so the house looks really good.

The huge first mosquitoes are just starting to come out, but they fly slow and make so much noise it is fairly easy to duck away from them. We take the picnic table and set it over to one side, then make some benches out of planks and cinder blocks. Rose has baked a cake and decorated it. The guys very carefully carried it over so it wouldn't get damaged and set it out on the table. We turned a large pan upside down over it to deter the jays.

Everyone gathered around and found places to sit on a bench. Rose stood in front and Noah beside her. I walked between the benches and Noah held out his hand to me. The look in his eyes left no doubt in me that this man loves me and I love him in return.

A marriage ceremony is so brief and means so much, changing a person's whole life in a few minutes and two simple little words.

I do.

There is much laughing and joking, with congratulations offered and accepted. Noah and I finish filling out the license and 2 people signed as witnesses. Rose signed it and we wrote it all in a large ledger book she brought from in her library. The page we kept and she would keep the ledger. She would try to record everything of interest in it. The birth of the twins, Dallas and Savannah was already in it. Now we are.

Kara and Rose also brought over a large meal they prepared earlier, with plates and utensils for everyone. So we had a wedding brunch and then some cake. A wonderful day. Everyone admired my ring set. With the 3rd ring entwined with the first two, it was a unique and unusual design.

By late afternoon, everyone headed back home and we were left alone. Married. We were married. To each other. I was very nervous now, but the house was clean, the dishes had gone home with Rose and Kara. The chores had been done and we were married.

Reality really hit me when Noah followed me into the house and on into the bedroom. Then he kissed me and the nervousness disappeared and the rest of the night was perfect.

There is a lot to be said for marriage. Waking up to magic fingers and nibbly kisses is one of them.

Later, we do the chores and milking. Any day now we should have some chicks hatching. Then in another week after that, the next batch of chicks. I have let half the hens stay broody. I want to have enough chickens to share with everyone that wants to keep some and raise their own. It will take a lot longer with the goats. Everyone has at least one or two dogs now, so we should do okay for working dogs in the future. Not so well for housecats. All we have out here are neutered. Now we just have to find a way to feed all of the animals as well as the people.

As the ground thaws, I am pulling small brush and weeds to enlarge the area my garden is in. I still have some vegetables left over in storage in my cellar under the house and I want to see if I replant the cabbage, if I can get seeds to save for the future. I place the potatoes out on the floor on the sun porch to warm and start sprouting better.

We scatter ashes all over the garden area and dump a lot of the barn cleanings into a large barrel to fill with water once it warms more and no chance of frost for the garden. All the weeds go in the barrel, also. The refuse from the chicken coop is too hot to use right in the garden, so we plan on digging the dirt out in the greenhouse and putting a deep layer of it in there, then covering with soil to heat the growing beds.

I thought we were ready for spring, but it still gets here before I am ready. Since it only lasts 10 days to 2 weeks, we really have to get busy on the planting and cutting firewood. This year we can still use the pickup to haul the wood up the hill, but we are going to have to learn to cut it and haul it by hand as soon as we run out of gas. We may try dragging wood home by wagon and save the gas as long as possible for the chainsaws. I can see we need more dogs to help on the pulling stuff around. Of course, more dogs means more food needed for them. A vicious cycle.

Al shows up a week or so later and has a very young caribou calf on his pack. While hiking, he found the cow down and dying and saved the calf but has no idea what to do with it now. Then he thought of us and our goat. So, we are now in possession of a very small caribou. I wonder how they are to train? Maybe if it is raised with the goats, we can train them all. Reindeer are domesticated caribou after all. If they can pull an old fat man around every year, they should be able to help around here. It is worth a try. The nanny isn't too thrilled with her new baby, but eventually allows it to nurse. It is hungry enough that as soon as the milk touches its mouth, it latches on.

We don't let it have too much to start, since it has missed several meals and might get scours from too much too fast. Plus I have no idea how rich caribou milk is or if it compares to goat milk.

Al says he finds baby animals quite often

and if we want to try doing anything with them, he will bring them by. This could be interesting.

Al also plans on moving up to the Yukon River for the summer salmon runs in July. He asks if any of the folks here would like to go and share in the fishing and the fish. Even if we don't want it for ourselves, we can use it for dog food. He uses his dogs as pack animals to haul their winter food home from the river after the fishing is done. Dried, he can load quite a lot of fish per dog pack. He has an area he fishes and stashes his nets there after he is done. This year, he will make travois for the dogs to pull so he can make it all in one trip. Noah asks if he can ask over at the other places to see if they want to go. He would love to but hates to leave me here by myself to take care of everything and just in case there is any trouble from stray folk still wandering around. Al is okay with that and says he has plenty of net and it is easier to fish with more than one or two people, especially now with no fuel. 3 people would be great, one to row the boat, one to tend net and one on the bank tending the fire and keeping animals away from the catch. They can trade off as they get tired of each job.

After Al leaves, we check on the baby caribou and she is curled up with the kid goat, sleeping. That should help the nanny accept her easier as she will now smell like the other baby.

Noah suggests we walk over and spread the news to see who wants to fish part of the summer. I want to stay and get the garden finished so he heads on over to see his Dad.

Chapter 3

After Noah leaves, I let the chickens out for a while in the little pen with wheels so I can move them around the yard and garden. It has a wire roof so hawks and owls can't have chicken dinner.

We have 30 chicks so far and they are doing well. The hens are very protective of the little balls of fluff, so I don't worry too much. But everything that would eat them is so much bigger than even the hens, I do worry some.

We have more than tripled the size of the garden this year and it is going to be a full time job taking care of it, since our lives pretty much depend on it now. I plant some of the feed grain I have left, hoping to be able to harvest it this fall, just by hand. We are getting a lot of animals that will all need hay and some grain. I can cut natural hay like I did last year. Barley and oats both grow well in Alaska, so I am hoping I get it right. Wheat isn't a very good crop for here or maybe I just didn't have the right type. I scatter grain and rake it in to keep the birds from eating it all.

Noah comes back much sooner than I expected. Jeremy has seen sign of someone hanging around and a bit of petty thievery.

We will have to be very careful from now on. There will be more survivors showing up and not all will be nice folks.

Thad will be one of the men going with Al to fish. Several of the others want to go, but they may have to draw straws. Only one more can go. It will probably be James, one of Kara's spare kids. He doesn't have family out here to take care of and he would like to go.

We make sure we have one of the dogs or more with each of us while we are working now. They will alert us to anyone around. I also lock the house whenever I am not in it. I don't want to be working in the garden, walk in the house and find someone waiting for me.

I string out barbed wire on plastic hooks around the barn and yard to the house. Then I hook it up to the electric fence charger I have from the ranch. It is supposed to handle 15 miles of fence. I only have about 250 feet so it should be strong. Then I hook it to an old Cat battery and that has a small solar panel trickle charging it all the time. The dogs will soon get used to it and so will we. It might deter a bear, also. Anyone or anything touching it will notice. There will also be a lot of noise, if past experience is anything to go by. Those barbs go through just about any clothes or fur.

Now that the animals are so important to

us, I can't take chances. Theft of food or animals is now a possible death sentence to anyone stolen from and certainly will be for the thief if caught.

I don't think anyone has a means of keeping a thief alive for punishment in some dim future, so I am thinking most will just bury them. I know I am not feeding and housing a thief. If someone asks and is willing to work for assistance, if I have extra I will help. Family and friends come first with sharing food, though.

We continue working on the firewood and gardens. The greenhouse is all planted now. We are showing progress.

The next trip over to see Rose and Kara, we box up a rooster and hen starting to act broody for her. She has a place to put them now and can start planting feed for them for winter. Maybe even get some chicks since the hen is broody. I take a container of fertile eggs with us. She can decide what she wants to do.

We don't stay long after giving her the chickens. With no one else to watch our place when we leave, we don't like leaving it empty.

When we get home, there are scraps of material on the barbs of the fence and the dogs are furious. I let them out and they sniff and trail all over the yard and fences. They start to go over the side of the bank at the edge of the yard by the woods, and we call them back.   Someone has definitely been here.

This is not something I want to deal with and I am sure Noah doesn't, either.   Nothing has grown enough in the garden or greenhouse to be stolen as food.   But our animals are vulnerable to any thief just wanting to butcher them and eat them.   The chickens are fairly safe once they are closed in for the night but while they are out in their pen, they are not.   Luckily we keep their pen inside the electric fenced area and this time it saved the day.

While we restring the fence they had torn loose, I tell Noah about the black bear I caught in it the last time I used it.

I was living here in a tent while building the first little cabin and for a chance for a decent night's sleep, I put the fence up around my area.   One night while asleep, I woke up to a racket that scared me half to death.   A medium sized black bear was caught in the wire and some of it came unhooked from the fence posts.   It coiled around him and he was not happy and squalling like fury.   When he finally tore loose, he was still squalling as he ran over the bank and off into the trees. There was a lot of fur but only a drop or two of blood left as evidence and a lot of tracks and torn up ground.   I don't think it ever came back.   I certainly slept better from then on, knowing the fence was there.

Noah was smiling by the time I was done with the story so I was smiling too. We looked at the house and went in for a while and then returned to work, smiling even more. Being married is better than I thought.

The caribou calf is growing and since the kid and nanny run to us for attention, so does she. We start putting small halters on both the little ones and leading them around by the halters while they are little enough that we can yard them around without hurting ourselves. Then we start putting something behind them to drag along while we lead them. After a while, we add long reins and walk behind and rein them right or left and voice commands at the same time. The calf is getting much larger than the kid so soon we will have to have another source of food for her. We do have a lot of lichen growing through the woods here, so maybe that will work. If she is used to eating hay from the start of winter, she should be able to eat it all winter, also.

Now that the goats and calf are used to the halters, we stake them out around the yard a lot to browse. The goats go for the brush and trees, the caribou likes the new grass. The chickens aren't fussy and eat anything that gets in front of them. They have caught a couple of the voles and even ate them. I guess it won't hurt the eggs or meat, but my chickens can be mean.

I am actually happy to see them eating the voles. They look like a short eared mouse and most folks just call them mice. But they will tunnel down a row of potatoes and leave nothing but the vines and a few roots. They will eat almost anything else, also. Then I saw a porcupine climb into the planter boxes I was raising my peas and beans in and eat the plants. I never even considered a porcupine as a garden pest. Then it turned and started humming. It hummed a 4 note song and kept repeating it. If I mimicked it, it turned and came over to me. How do you shoo off a friendly humming porcupine? I bought fine mesh chicken wire and strung it around the bottom of my fence line around the garden. The fence only seems to keep out hares and porcupines. Everything else just steps over it. If I had more barbed wire, I would string it around the entire garden area and the grain, also.

I read somewhere about building an earth battery. I am not sure if it really works, but talk it over with Noah. He figures it is worth the effort to try it, if we can find enough materials. He will go see his Dad and see what he thinks. I am staying home and not leaving the place undefended.

This time, nothing happens while Noah is gone, but I still breathe a sigh of relief when he gets home. It may be as much from no one showing up here or just that he has made the trip safely.

He says his Dad is intrigued by the idea and will see what he has of the materials needed. If it works, he will try making one for each place. It would solve some of our light problems in winter. With the 12 volt LED lights every home could be well lit during the times most needing light. The uses are limitless.

Chapter 4

One day while we are working outside, we hear an airplane. It turns out to be the same fellow that came late in the winter. He has switched from skis over to balloon tires. He decided after going home that gas was only going to be good for flying for a limited time anyway, so he would just as soon go see what town looked like and take his chances.

He is looking for 2 guys to ride with him to Fairbanks, to see what is left and if there are any supplies at all available. Noah would like to go, but doesn't want to take a chance leaving me and maybe never making it back. Jeremy was over at Romans and when everyone shows up, several other guys volunteer, but Jeremy and one other ex-military fellow go with the pilot. The other guy has pilot experience so if anything happens, they can possibly make it home. Each person including the pilot is loaded with weapons. If anyone does see them get out of the plane, they are apt to think they are under attack. If anyone is around where they land, they may have a tough time getting the plane back off the ground.

They decide one person will stay with the plane at all times and the other 2 will scout around. They each have body armor and a large backpack, empty.   There are survival rations in the plane.

We wish them well and they take off for town or whatever is left there, now.

We visit for a while with the others that came to see the plane and finally share some lunch.

Many hours later, we hear a plane coming in.   When they land, they look exhausted. Jeremy walks over to me, cradling something in his arms.   He found a bedraggled looking female cat and just couldn't leave her.   She did not have much left of her ears and some of her tail must have frozen off, also.   But she was purring and friendly.   When I started to take her into the house, she was not calm about that.   I took her out to the barn and somehow the presence of the other animals soothed her enough to allow me to place her near the leftover pile of hay in the loft.

When I walked back over to the men, a lot of the talking stopped, so I figured I could get the details later from Noah and went back to the barn.   I placed a pan of water and some food for the cat up in the loft.   She was already munching on one of my nemesis voles so I knew we would get along fine.   She was super skinny, but as I petted her, I discovered she was also pregnant, so there was at least one more cat still alive in the town area.

The pilot decides not to try flying home tonight.   He is worn out so we invite him to

stay in our little cabin. We go in and I fix
dinner while the guys continue talking.

He said it is terrible in town. There was
little damage from the earthquake, but it looks
like most of town had burned to the ground.
Whole neighborhoods were burned also.
They did a quick flyover of the town and
found some areas not burned where
businesses had been located. They landed
out a ways from anything so no one could
sneak up on them.

They hiked to the industrial area and found
the rods we had asked for. Then they looked
around a bit and found small cylinders of
oxygen and acetylene. The pilot found a
shop that sold ATVs and got one started so
started ferrying stuff out to the plane. They
loaded a small trailer they found and hooked
to the ATV and parked it out where they
could get the stuff if they try another trip to
town. They did find fuel at the ATV dealers
place, so topped off the planes' tanks.

They used the ATV and went around
where grocery stores used to be. They were
all burned out. They did make one discovery
that was good news for us. The nursery
south of town was still standing and had a lot
of plants that survived the winter and also a
lot of seeds so they loaded up the ATV with
all they could haul out and the backpacks were
full. The seeds were brought this trip and the
tanks would be picked up tomorrow. They

had wrapped small shrubs and trees in plastic and tarps and that was the bundles all over the outside of the plane. Probably not aerodynamic, but it made it okay. The pilot said he had a nice place up the Porcupine but no neighbors at all and he could not grow much variety as his growing season was worse than ours. He wanted to know if he could move here to our area and build a place.

Well, I would think it would be okay. We should all probably talk it over and not just say yes, but I see no problem. It isn't like anyone is going to complain that he is on their property as most was State or Federally owned before.

We are all up early in the morning and finish unloading the plane and unwrapping the bundles on the outside, too. Jeremy and the other fellow are back for another run to town. Rose and Kara have walked over and we sort through the seeds, we will divide them into things it is still early enough to plant this year. The small trees and other perennials we sort out and water. Most had been in pots that were left as being too heavy and the roots are still damp as the men had wrapped them quite well. But they will need immediate attention or they won't survive the trauma of being bare root while starting to grow leaves. We know they are hardy to have survived this winter with no care at all. We place the apples in one area and cover the roots well to protect them, and the plums and cherries in other piles. The service berries and Mt. Ash are separated, and there are a few mystery plants we haven't a clue about as the labels didn't seem to make it.

There are gooseberries, currants, and some other mystery plants there, also. The mints are certainly welcome additions for all our places.

When the plane comes back today, there are a few more surprises for us all. The pilot found another goat. It did not enjoy riding in a plane and made it known by biting a chunk out of the seat. For the time being, we placed her over in the fenced area near the barn. Jeremy came back but the other fellow was trying to bring a 6 wheeled ATV pulling a trailer of stuff they had salvaged.

So far, they had not found a single living person. There were vehicles clogging the roads heading south from Fairbanks for miles, and it looked like most had perished inside their rigs. The early winter storm catching them unprepared and either dying from cold or carbon monoxide from idling the motors for warmth. There were human remains all over town. Just bundles of rags over bones. Nothing to be identified.

They had stopped back by the nursery and loaded up even more of the plants they could find that sounded like food. The pilot thought if he could find an area here, he would like to start a nursery or mainly grow food. Everyone seemed to think that was a great idea and we all could help him get a place built.

The pilot wanted to go back and get another load, since he was able to fuel up each trip. He thought he could bring enough to help him get started. Another volunteer joined the pilot and Jeremy went with him, to help. Jeremy was leery because they were landing in the same place each time they went and if anyone was watching the area, a plane is hard to not notice when it is the only one in the sky. He finally convinced the pilot to land in a different area and they carefully approached the area they stashed the ATV the night before. A movement off to the right caught Jeremy's eye and he pointed out the ambush to the pilot. They backed away silently and went directly back to the plane to find there were a couple of fellows intent on acquiring the plane. Jeremy went to work and soon they were in the air heading to the other side of town. A quick touch down by the nursery on the street and they loaded as much as they could of the greenhouse kits and fertilizers. Then to the building supply store. More movement in the ruins caught their eye, so they just came on home. They did see the 6 wheeler ATV on its way out with the load from yesterday. It should arrive late this afternoon.

There was a nice bench of land just beyond Will and Shari's place that would be easy to clear and build on. After looking it over, the pilot, Dan Hiller, asked if it was okay if he laid claim and staked it out. None of us objected and some of the men went over to help clear the ground.

They could hear the ATV before it came into view on the roadway. Dan met it where his drive would be and they pulled in to start unloading most of the building supplies here.

Some of the young women that came out with Sam offered to assemble some of the greenhouse kits and get some plants going as it was still early enough to grow some crops. Soon, there was a very small Trapper style cabin up and 3 of the greenhouses. The girls placed them in a row, so some of the plastic rolls could be added over it all and have a long narrow greenhouse out of the whole works. This almost doubled the growing area for this season. They planned on coming back tomorrow and spading up the ground between the greenhouses to start planting. Seeds were set soaking overnight to speed their growth, also.

The cabin was all green logs, so it was not going to be the best place to winter in and would be shrinking and settling. But it would give some protection for the summer from the elements. Once Dan got settled in, he could start a real home and this could be an outbuilding. In a pinch, it could be lived in year around.

While everyone sat around relaxing after dinner and a good day's work, talk turned to the ambushers in town. No shots were fired, only clubs and knives had been seen. The areas of town that were burned out seemed to be the areas with food and weapons for sale. We may never know if someone burned them to cover their trail or if it was accidental. For certain, there was not much left of the main part of town. The fellows seemed to think they could wait a few days or weeks and then go back and get more stuff. It did not seem like a very good idea to me. Someone may be watching now that they knew others survived and had a plane. There may be other good things where the plane came from. They may start looking for us now. I really didn't want that. I voiced my concerns to Noah and he agreed with me. He brought that up with the guys when they were working the next day, but everyone seemed to think we were far enough out to be safe.

To me, one trip was safe, two trips was pressing their luck and three trips was asking for trouble. If they could get ATVs running and out here, so could others. Jim brought the load over the rotten ice on the rivers he crossed to get here, yesterday, so that would not be a safe option soon. It probably was not a safe option yesterday when he was doing it. He had found a few more items to add to his load as he passed the building supply yards and had been vastly overloaded for the whole trip.

Dan decided he had enough gas to go back to get the rest of his stuff on the Porcupine, so left the next morning.

Sam and her friends still went down most days to get a good garden ready for Dan. One of the women, Melanie, seemed to be very interested in Dan. The others were not that interested in gardening, but she kept them at it.

Dan was so overloaded when he returned, everyone wondered how he managed to get it airborne to start with. He laughed and said his runway was on a bluff, so when he went off the end, he had a lot of area to get it going. He always waited for the wind sock to show an updraft there. The FAA would certainly not approve of his loading techniques. That poor plane looked like a loaded down pack mule. Building supplies and food, with food making up most of the load. The inside of the plane was loaded with food, the building supplies were strapped on the outside. Windows, a door, some roofing and some plywood. I marveled that the plane ever lifted at all. He said he had enough gas for a trip to town if they could fill up in town to get back, but not enough to go back to the Porcupine for another load.

I talked to Noah about us giving Dan enough gas for another load from his home. He had been more than fair in bringing stuff for everyone out from town. A lot of these supplies would make life easier for all of us in the long run. We decided yes, we could do that.

Dan walked over to see if we minded keeping his goat a while longer as he did not have any place for her. We asked him if he wanted to wait until next year to have her have a kid or would he want to milk all winter and take care of the little one also. If she were bred now, she would birth in 5 months so it would be October, early November and the weather can be extremely cold then unless he had a barn ready before then. He thought it over a while and asked how I would like another goat. Uuuh, I didn't see that coming.

I guess that would be really nice, and we are set up for it. Then Noah asks him if he wants to go back to the Porcupine for his last load. We have gas, depending on how much he would need. He says another 5 gallons would give him enough to make the trip home and he still has some gas left there. He hikes back and taxis the plane back to our driveway. Noah pours the fuel in and Dan is on his way back to the Porcupine.

We put our new goat in with the billy and now we will have year around milking to do. I better start making cheese and experimenting more. We will have enough for everyone to have milk and cheese if I can do it.

I'm going to have a sore shoulder from patting myself on the back if I don't watch it.

Dan returns the next day, again vastly overloaded. He says he only left the shell of a house there and nothing at all of any use to anyone. As we help him unload, I think he is probably right. He wants to park the plane here and is using the 6 wheeled ATV and trailer to haul his stuff home. He left a few more traps for me to include for my trapline next winter. I may set them inside the outbuildngs and the ice house to make sure no rodents take up residence. I don't want to catch our barn cat. She is recovering quite well with regular meals and is looking very good, in spite of very short ears and tail. She has a dense underfur and that is probably all that kept her alive over the winter last year. She is a large cat and very friendly. She washes the faces of the kid and the calf after they nurse. It is fun to watch her with the other animals. She herds the baby chicks, trying to keep them close to the barn and house. One day she comes into the yard, working hard to herd a flock of baby grouse. The mother is squawking trying to entice the babies back. She gets the grouse into the pen with the hens and chicks and is so proud of herself. The hens aren't sure about added chicks, but what the heck, one clucks over them, plumping herself down and all the chicks cuddling under her. Evidently, the grouse aren't adverse to a warm nap no matter who they nap under. By the next day, most have gone back to their mother but 2 stay with the chickens.

Chapter 5

We are all in full work mode now. The ice has gone out of the rivers and they are in full flood. It won't last too long as we have not had any rain, so it is just snow melt runoff. We take some of the berry bushes Dan brought out over for Al. We hadn't seen him in quite a while and wanted to make sure he was okay.

We halloo'd the house as we walked in so we wouldn't startle him. He yells back that he is out back, so we walk around the end of his cabin. He crawls out from under the corner of his cabin where he was repairing an old support post.

We ask if he would like the plants and a few of the other ones we have extra at the house. He starts smiling and says, "You bet I would. I have been torturing myself thinking I will never taste these things again in my life."

He decides to plant the future little apple trees against his house and espalier them to increase the chances they will survive and produce. Might even be able to keep the moose from eating them, there. The moose are my main worry also. They totally love apple trees, even crabapple trees. They keep my crabapples chewed down to stumps.

He doesn't have any strawberry plants either, so I offer him some of my plants as starts and they make lots of runners. He can make a whole bed that way.

We visit a while, then head home. The next morning, Noah wakes me to breakfast in bed. It is our 1 month anniversary. He even found a small flower somewhere to place on the make shift tray he brought in. Aw, what a sweetheart.

After breakfast, we do the chores and he goes to cut wood while I weed in the garden. I wheel the chicken pen in between rows so they can weed and fertilize and bug control all in one for me. There are so many chicks now it is hard to keep track. The older ones are getting feathers started on their wings and look odd. When a hen plops down and starts calling chicks for naps, no matter who mom is, several manage to get in under her. The 2 grouse chicks manage to settle in well whenever there is a nap time.

The added animal fertilizer is making a major difference in how the greenhouse and garden are doing. Everything is growing so fast I can almost sit and watch it grow. I mix up manure tea and spray it over the areas I planted the oats and barley seed. This will mean the difference in whether all our animals make the winter or not and whether we manage to live quite well or just survive, ourselves.

There is going to be another wedding. Jeremy and Ashley are getting married and want to stake a parcel of land between Will and Shari and Rose.   We plan another cabin building.   Nothing fancy, just another Trappers cabin like we built for Dan.   At least it will give them a start and privacy.   We are getting quite a little community going here.

One of the other women that came out with Sam has her eye on Dan.   He doesn't seem particularly interested in her but is polite and friendly.

He stays at his place, working on making it winter livable and growing enough so he can survive in fairly good comfort.   He adds a chicken coop onto his cabin, similar to mine and I give him a hen and rooster.   Some of the chicks are able to be shared out also, so he gets a couple of them but I am not positive if they are pullets or roosters yet.   I think they are pullets.   Once they start laying in the fall, he should have some eggs most of the winter if he keeps them warm and well fed and watered.   Some extra light in the early morning should help also.

The ground is thawed deep enough now for the guys to attempt building an earth battery.   They start at our place and soon have a grid of copper and galvanized rods pounded down 2 feet in a 2 feet apart grid.   Then fastened together with electrical wire and hooked to a multi meter to check.   The amps are not up enough, so they do another parallel grid beside the first.   It takes a while, but after a lot of pounding and testing, they think they have it figured out.

I have some 12 volt LED lights that truckers used to use to fancy up the trucks. I dig them out and the men test it out on them. YES, it works. It's a good thing I am such a packrat. I think I should put a strip in the ice house and one in the middle of my house to use instead of my propane. Then I can save the propane for the cook stove. I am not looking forward to not being able to use it in the future.

We place a strip in the barn and it handles all of them very well. This will help us a lot on what we can do in future. I don't know how long it takes the galvanized zinc to wear off the rods, but we have a lot of them and pieces of galvanized old water pipe. Maybe that will work, also.

It doesn't take much to operate only 3 or 4 of the little LED lights, so the men make smaller set ups at the little cabins at Rose's. For Kara and Rose, they fix one each like mine. Then on down to Will and Shari then Dan's. They stop to see if Jeremy has an idea yet of where he wants his cabin, then proceed to put in a battery for him. Thad and Noah take the rods needed and some LED lights and wire over to Al's place and fix him up with a set, before the battery making is over. This should help us all in winter. It will save on supplies, also.

Chapter 6

Down in Oregon, when the earthquake hit, Rose's sister and family did not have much damage to their remote area. However, with the larger population in the immediate area, even though by most standards it was thinly populated, they had more problems with thievery and intruders. Within a month, they knew they needed to move, so started preparing.

By the end of the first winter, they decided to attempt a move north, using horses and driving as many cattle as they could round up. They figured if it could be done during the Gold Rush era, they could do it now. One family that lived near them wanted to come along also. So did a few good friends. So they had enough riders to handle a fairly large herd of horses and cattle.

Liz used to train horses for harness work and they built a good sturdy wagon to haul things that couldn't or shouldn't be packed on horses. She figured if they had to drop things along the way, it would just be a redo of the old days on that, also.

Her husband, Richard, was handy with tools and repairs, so was the neighbor, Mike. The men decided on what tools they would definitely have to have to keep everything in good condition and maybe be able to construct things as needed, later. They rounded up all the hand tools they could find and materials to build wood gasifiers, later. They built one to see how it would work and hooked it up to one of the older model 4 wheel drive farm tractors in the area. They could cut wood along the way to keep it running and it could pull a larger load of supplies.

They used maps to decide which route would possibly be better for the trip although the maps were no longer very accurate. With all the animals, equipment and people, they did not want to attempt any large gorges or the rivers at their widest. So they decided to swing east a bit, maybe find their oldest daughter and her family and miss Hell's Canyon and the Columbia after the Snake River joined it.

They knew they would be doing good to make 12 to 20 miles a day, and since it was almost 3000 miles, the way they planned on going, they had to plan on traveling up to 3 years to reach Rose's area. So enough food, clothing and camping gear had to be accumulated. By early spring they were ready to start.

After they left their valley, they found few places with anyone living in them. Along the way, horses and cattle joined in the herd they were pushing along, until it almost doubled in size. Somewhere, a couple more dogs joined the herd, and acted like they knew what they were doing and were welcome.

The dogs alerted them to the danger before anyone noticed some men hiding in the rocks. In the small squirmish that followed, a couple of her crew received bullet grazes, but no bad injuries, which couldn't be said for the would-be thieves. As soon as they fired the first shot, they were met with deadly accuracy in the return fire. They were left lay to feed the buzzards and coyotes.

They did not push the herd as it had to feed enough along the way to survive. Liz had old topo maps with her and so far, they were still accurate. She did not know how long that would last, but thanked God for it and to see them through.

By the time they skirted the remains of Ontario on the Idaho border, they developed a routine for the day.

They found an area of extremely good grazing, so Liz and Richard left the herd to rest for the day and took spare horses to see about finding Lori and family. They were surprised to find them fairly easily and by late evening, returned to camp with them and their gear.

One of the kids found an abandoned storage cellar still packed full of potatoes, so they loaded up every available space with them and bags of storage carrots that were on one side in the building. They would not last long, but it would extend their food supplies quite well. Marsha and Liz planted some out beside the cellar to keep some available to anyone in the future that came by and prayed others would find the stored ones before they spoiled.

As they wended their way up Idaho, they found other abandoned storage facilities and restocked at every opportunity. The dried bean warehouse was a great discovery. They planted some out near the buildings and loaded down their wagons to the limit.

They kept a large container of beans soaking while traveling, changing the water when they found water, to practically presprout the beans, then they only took a short time to cook in the evenings when they stopped and started a fire first, then set up camp. A pot of potatoes started with the beans would make a filling meal. By evening, the cattle and horses were usually tired enough to settle down and rest and graze a bit all night.

The grass was growing well by this time in their travels and they wanted to get as many miles behind them as possible before winter set in again. They did not know how they were going to feed so many animals all winter, but figured that was a future problem, only handle the day to day problems now.

By the time they crossed into Canada, everyone was well seasoned to the saddle and the routine. Going up the Okanogan Valley, they found deserted orchards and only signs of a few people here and there. They did find one family settled in and making a go of it. They traded a few of the cows with younger calves that needed rest and a couple of the spare horses that had joined along the way. They gave him a bag of the potatoes to add a different variety to what he had growing.

The man had bags of dried fruits he and his family prepared last year and since crops were not ready yet now, it was a good addition to the diet of the trail drivers. One of the cows traded, looked like she had some milk cow in her and if he could train her to allow milking, he would have milk for his family. She was already with calf for next season, so he should be okay.

While camped up the valley from him, one of their herd broke a leg in a bog hole and they put it down and butchered it out. They pegged out the hide to dry overnight and sliced the meat into thin strips to dry on poles over the fire. The farmer rode up as they were eating dinner, having heard the shot. They told him he was welcome to the thin pickings of the remains and a front quarter, sorry they didn't have more to share. He gathered up the head, bones and quarter and took them home. It would make soup and fresh meat for a while for them.

They tried to stay on the east side of the rivers as far north as they could, so when they finally had to cross, maybe it wouldn't be so wide and deep.

By the time they reached the Quesnel area and turned west, the weather was turning chilly and they knew they better find an area to spend the worst of it. What they found exceeded their wildest dreams.

When they crested the hill and first saw the giant barns mostly still standing, they thought it was a mirage. Then as they got closer and found that they were real and full of hay, they were cautious. No sign of anyone having been there for a very long time. No trails through the tall grass growing all around the buildings. Fences partly standing, but no repairs. The main house was partly burned, but could be repaired sufficiently to use.

The cattle and horses poured through the break in the fence onto the fields and settled right in, eating. The crew repaired the fence right behind them. Then some rode each direction and repaired any downed fence as they found it. Tonight, maybe everyone would get a full night's sleep. There was a large orchard behind the buildings and it was fully loaded with fruit. The canned food in the house were mostly not usable, having frozen and broke last winter. But there were cases of empty canning jars and lids in the pantry.

There were chickens running around out in the trees behind the house and barns. The kids were given the task of catching as many as they could.   They found some fish nets hanging in the barn and planned ways to catch a lot of chickens.   They would keep as many as possible and have eggs part of the winter, but there were enough chickens to have a chicken dinner for the group now and then, also.

Everyone got busy on preparing for the winter fast approaching.   The orchard was picked clean the day after they arrived.   Two nights later, there was a frost.   Indoors, they were cleaning, slicing and drying as much of the fruit as possible while eating quite a bit of it fresh.   Pies were made and enjoyed.

There was enough hay and feed in the barns to keep the herd quite well for the winter.   The chicken coop was repaired and as the kids caught chickens, they were returned to the coop.   One old hen had a late hatch of chicks and they were eventually all caught and put in the coop, also.

The first Sabbath after settling in was indeed a day of Thanksgiving, so an appropriate meal had been prepared the day before and the day was spent giving thanks for all they had received.   They were set for the winter and could resupply a lot of their needs for the rest of the trip north.

Chapter 7

Meanwhile, Rose had no idea her sister and family were moving north. Everyone proceeded on preparing for winter, even though it was early summer yet.

Since the little snack shack would not be used as a snack shack in the foreseeable future, the pass throughs were removed, one filled with insulation and a window put in the other. It didn't have a way to heat it, but it was insulated. A bunk bed was built into the end of it and a very small wood stove and chimney near the door after the sink was removed. The door was covered in foam board to insulate it a bit, too, since it was an old military surplus screen door. It had some insulation, but not much. It would give a person a place alone if they wanted away from everyone a while.

The partially built house on the north edge of her property was finished with an upstairs and Kevin and his group moved into it. Then they started cutting firewood for the winter. Sam and her group wanted their own house, also, so moved for the time being into the small guest cabin. Her son wanted to stay with grandma, so he could always be found down at Kara's. Usually Kevin's son was there, also.

Paul and Jenna had their own place they built a couple of years ago. Finally, Kara had her home back, just in time to have to share it again. She or Rose did the cooking for everyone for the evening meal. There was no room for negotiation on that, there was not enough food for anyone to get picky or quibble about what they wanted for dinner. Breakfast was the same, only food was sent to each house and it had to last the month. If someone got greedy, the household took care of the problem. Not everyone was happy, but they were alive and had shelter and food.

Jeremy and Ashley's wedding would be at Will and Shari's home. Their homes were fairly close together and from an upstairs window in Will and Shari's house, they could see upstairs windows in both Dan's and Jeremy's houses. They worked out colored signals to place in the windows in case anyone needed help. Most of the time a green cloth was over those windows, and if help needed, a red cloth was to be hung. If anyone just wanted company, they hung a blue cloth. If ill, yellow.

One morning they saw a red flag at Dan's so rushed over with guns, only to find that he was color blind, so they wrote on his flags what color each one was. He was a little sheepish about it and never told anyone. Then he found out both Kevin and Paul were, also.

On one of Jeremy's jaunts in the woods, he found an old snow machine, abandoned, out of gas. It had some items on it that made him think it was the means of Royal showing up out here during the winter. He searched around the snow machine in ever widening circles and finally found Royal's remains. There was not enough left to actually identify, but there was no coat but a lot of winter gear on the rest of the body.

Now we could relax a bit about Royal, just not too much in case anyone else came with evil intentions.

Shari made a lovely cake for the wedding. She experimented with the birch syrup and the frosting was a creation from that. The wedding was nice, but everyone was delighted by the cake. There were not many sweet treats on menus now. I gave them a small bag of the candy I made in my experiment and they sampled it immediately, but saved it to have on hand.

No one wanted to leave their property unattended very long, so get-to-gethers were usually very short. We enjoyed seeing everyone, we talked fast, we went home. It is one way to make sure you stay friends with your neighbors and no one outstayed their welcome. Works for me.

Al's dog had 8 puppies and he doesn't want to take them all to fish camp. So he brings the dog and pups to me. He and Thad have their supplies in their backpacks and each takes a pack dog to help bring home what they hope will be large quantities of dried salmon. It is a good 2 day walk to the Yukon

River if they don't dawdle.

Al drew out a map for us to come check if they are not back in a month. He hopes to catch enough during the first run to last us for dog food all winter with some prepared as strips for people to enjoy. They expect to have to make several trips or if they do well, for others to go back with them to retrieve the rest. Will offers them his 6 wheeler, but no one wants to use gas unless necessary. They may use it to bring fish home if they have success. Then Dan hears about it and volunteers to fly it if they need it for larger payload and less gas.

We put Al's dog and puppies in one of the pens. She is not used to goats, caribou calves and chickens wandering around and may decide they would be a good lunch for her and her pups. There is a shelter in one corner in case of rain.

Soon, the grass starts making seed heads, so it is time to start cutting grass again. I start out slower this year with the scythe. Still sore muscles but not as bad. Noah takes a turn at it and is surprised how soon he is feeling the affects. I have a sickle, also, but having to bend over so low to cut near the ground is killing my back. I may try it for harvesting the grains when they get more mature.

Soon some of the berries are getting ripe, and we have to race the bears for them. We have wild raspberries, wild red currants, wild blueberries and domestic strawberries. Later, there will be low bush cranberries or lingonberries to pick. I find a large enough patch of cloud berries to pick some for a batch of jelly. They are very short plants with only one berry per plant, so those are not something we spend a lot of time looking for. I do pick some half ripe high bush cranberries for jelly. Half ripe, they taste similar to apple jelly and I add some mint leaves to make it even better. Once they are ripe, they have a musty flavor and smell that I can't stomach. Old sweat socks come to mind. Not my idea of a pleasant addition to any meal.

Dan decides he has waited long enough to try another trip to town, so Jeremy and Jim go with him. This trip is uneventful but they can see signs that someone has been to the places they salvaged from, before. They do find enough fuel to fill the plane first.

Two of the bridges across the Chena River have collapsed, so they have to look around to see what is safe. They do not touch anything that looks like anyone may be using it, but they do salvage items left around and no sign of anyone in the area doing anything with them.

They decide to check out one or two of the boat shops along the river and find a nice riverboat they both like. If necessary, it can be paddled. There is enough fuel in the outbuildings and oil to fill the tanks and haul extra along. They move the plane over near the boat and Jeremy and Jim will take the boat, while Dan loads up the plane with extra items from the shop for repairing motors. They place an extra motor and a kicker on the boat, Dan takes off in the plane and Jeremy and Jim head down the Chena to the Tanana. There were some river maps in the shop, so they have a fair idea of how to reach the Tolovana and Tatalina.

By the time they leave town, they are sure they will never come back just to search for things. It appears others may be in the area and also salvaging and they don't want to take something someone else is claiming.

The Tanana seems deeper and wider than they expected and when they reached the Tolovana, they had a hard time picking it out as they were in an extremely wide river by that time. They located it by the change in current coming in from the side, and turned to follow it. The lower end of the river they thought was the Tatalina was also wide and fairly deep. As they progressed, they could see salmon in the river under them, when they reached the clear water areas. They decided to attempt dip netting them with quite a bit of success. Now they were glad they had fastened the nets along the outside of the boat and had laughed when Dan asked if they expected to go to Chitina any time soon.

No one had walked down to the river from any of our places, since breakup. So none of us expected the boat to make it clear up the river to the old bridge site. Jim stayed with the boat and Jeremy walked up to Will's. They brought the 6 wheel ATV and trailer down to unload the boat. The fish went first. Since Rose and I had smokehouses, they brought us the fish and kept one at each house for fresh fish.

Soon, we were all cleaning fish, except Kara. She is extremely allergic and even the smell makes her swell and stop breathing. We started fish marinating immediately. Tomorrow, the smoking would start at both places. We dug trenches to bury the fish remains for future fertilizer. There would have to be a bear watch started 24/7. We could not afford to lose any food to bears. Besides, now they should be prime for butchering, themselves. We could use more cured hams and substitute bacon.

Early the third morning, the first bear joined the curing process. It was a very large fat bear, so we cut the meat and fat from over the ribs to use as bacon, the shoulders as picnic hams, the hams as, well, hams. The lower legs were cured to smoke for ham hocks. The few remaining pieces were made into roasts and BBQ ribs.

By the third bear, we were hoping for no more bears. But we took care of the meat and hides anyway. The smokehouses were very busy with the fish and after cleaning them, the bear meat was cured and ready to smoke.

Noah and I were walking over to check on Al's house every couple of days and watering his garden, greenhouse and taking care of his chickens. We weeded a bit now and then, also. As we were coming out his drive one evening, we met him coming in. He had one of the dogs and his backpack were both loaded with dried fish. We walked back in with him and helped unload. He was very tired and was hiking back the next day. So we handed him the bag of salmon strips we were carrying to snack on. He stopped mid-sentence and wanted to know how we got them. So we told him. He had never seen any salmon this close to home. He thought maybe he and Thad should come home and bring some of his nets to see if they could get enough fish here, to feed the dogs all winter. Maybe build a fish trap, since the Tatalina was not usually a very large volume river with a mild breakup. Maybe a community project to build a fish wheel. His head was buzzing with ideas and not having to make such a long hike any more unless he wanted to.

He said he and Thad had probably enough dried salmon already to last the winter for the dogs. Thad was still fishing, cutting and drying while he packed home. He decided to walk on down and talk to Dan about coming up with the plane to pick up the rest of the fish and maybe their gear if there is room. He also says he has a surprise for all of us.

We walk together to our driveway and he won't even give a clue about his surprise. After we finish up our chores for the evening, we concentrate on repairing the little weed whacker Roman loaned me last year. Finally, it is running again and we do just a little bit of grass and clover cutting which is twice as much as we managed with the scythe. My little dinky Scots uncle used to cut his entire hay meadows using one of those. Then he used homemade rakes to rake it all up. Those were so heavy it makes me tired just thinking about when we would go help rake and put up hay with him. After a day of working with him, I was always happy to go back to working on our place. We at least had store bought rakes that were less than half the weight of the homemade ones.

The next morning after chores, I start with the weed whacker again. I know someday soon I won't be able to use it ever again, and I want to get as much cut as possible before that happens.

While I am working, Dan flies over and wags his wings as he passes, heading north to the river. Al and his dog are with him. When he flies back later, he is alone but his plane is packed to the nth degree with stuff strapped all over the outside of the plane, also. He lands on the stretch of road just beyond our place and offloads a couple of the huge bales of fish. These will be for our dogs. Then he taxis down the road and drops more fish at Rose's driveway.

Since there probably will not be any traffic on the road, he just keeps taxiing down the road and drops more at Jeremy's then Will's. By the time he reaches his house, he just has his share left in the plane and the odor.

He wouldn't comment on the surprise Al was talking about and we were left to wonder.

A couple of days later, Al, Thad and 2 women walked in the driveway. As surprises go, this really is a surprise alright. Thad stays away from the one woman but Al lets the other one hang onto his arm. He introduces them, the one on his arm is Natalie, the other one is Amy. They were netting fish just a little ways upstream from Al's location and have no one else. He really liked the one woman but Thad was not interested in the other one at all. Al offered to let them stay at his place with him and they both accepted. They each had a large pack of supplies and Thad and Al both had packed even more of their supplies, all of which were now at Al's place. Thad said his goodbyes and walked on home and Al picked up his dog and pups and they went back the way they came.

As we smoked the fish and then the bear,

we hung everything in my larger ice house.   It would stay cool and no rodents or bugs would get into it.   I opened the vents to allow fresh air to circulate so no mold would start on the food.   It was really too early to start looking for a moose or caribou unless it was just standing there in the yard saying "shoot me."

The gardens were starting to produce, so we were all busy picking, canning and drying vegetables.   I was busy cutting and hauling hay, so was Noah.   If I was cutting with the weed whacker, he was using the scythe.   We both were getting much better with that scythe.

The barley and oats were starting to head very well, so we had to keep watch so it wouldn't just drop the seeds before we could harvest.   The wheat wasn't as advanced as the other grains.

Chapter 8

As I am doing chores the next morning, I

see a flash of movement out of the side of my eye and whirl around, gun drawn. Amy lets out a gasp and falls on her butt. I hold the gun down at my side and ask her what she is doing sneaking around. She gets all huffy and starts on about just coming to visit. I tell her, "No, don't give me that crap. If you were coming to visit, you would be walking in on the driveway, not sneaking out through the brush and bugs. If you want to visit, fine, come visit, but if you are sneaking around, expect to get shot."

She keeps the huffy attitude and I give her a kick in the butt as she flounces by. I couldn't help myself. I'm afraid she is going to be more trouble in the future and may wish I had just gone with my first instinct which was to shoot her.

When she gets back to Al's, she gives him some cock and bull story about me assaulting her. So he marches her right back over, with Natalie tagging along behind, to find out what really happened. Yup, I should have just shot her.

Al tells her to repeat what she has told him. She hems and haws around it and finally says I assaulted her and she wants me punished. I look at her in amazement. A kick in the butt is assault now? After what she had been calling me under her breath as she walked by, I should have smacked her around really good. She claims I hit her. So

I walk over and slug her as hard as I can. OWWW, not in the jaw, not in the jaw, I may have broken my hand. She drops like a bag of rocks. I look at Al and say, "yes, I hit her."

Natalie is speechless. I then tell them exactly what had happened here earlier in the day and that she was lucky I had not shot her. It turns out Natalie only knew her slightly before the quake and they teamed up after as they did not know if anyone but them had survived. She tended to shirk on the work needed to survive and always took a bit more than her share, but she was another human and Natalie just didn't want to be alone, entirely, as far as she knew.

We had no idea what to do with her now. Leeches and sneaks are not good to have around in hard times and these times qualified and so did she.

After a while, she started coming around. She gingerly touched her jaw and moved it around a bit. It wasn't broken, darn, now she could still talk.

She stood up and dusted herself off. She smiled and stuck out her hand to shake mine. What the heck? She said, "All my life, I have just inched by on what I could wheedle or sneak away from folks. You just called me and I do believe you may have also shown me the error of my ways."

I don't believe this and it is clear no one else does either. I shook her hand and told her, "If you ever so much as attempt any of that around here, someone will fill you full of holes so fast you won't know what hit you."

My hand is throbbing but not broken so I don't let on that it hurts like crazy to shake her hand. She is a bit subdued as she follows Al and Natalie home. I don't think Natalie or Al are going to cut her much slack from now on.

Over at Rose's, they have all been working, getting enough firewood for everyone for the coming winter. Food and firewood are the all-consuming topics of speech and work. Not enough of either one and someone may not survive the winter so both are very serious subjects.

They are also cutting seed heads of grass for the chickens, plus quite a bit of hay. They have a few rabbits that will need feed all winter also. They can cut brush to augment the rabbit's diet, but the chickens need grain to continue laying. We don't know what some of the wild grasses are, but they have nice seed heads and the chickens love them. We all fill buckets of fine gravel and keep it for the chickens and to use as kitty litter in the winter. Even the children are helping on gathering for winter.   Isaac being the oldest is the foreman and the other children are his crew.

He sets quotas for them and then rewards them with play time. He is excellent with them and very patient. Everyone tries not to make him take care of them all day so he can learn to work with the grownups, too. He is doing well at both jobs.

Here at home, we are getting a bumper crop from the garden. Between the weather staying nice and the homegrown fertilizer everything is growing fast and large. The barn cat is extremely good at catching the voles, so we are not losing much to them this year. Her kittens are learning right along with her. We cuddle and play with the kittens as much as possible and take them in the house often. My 2 are not amused by this but tolerate them. I don't want the kittens to live outdoors all the time as outdoor cats have a very short life expectancy in Alaska, between the weather and the predators. It seems that every household wants a cat, so there is no lack of homes for the kittens. Once the kittens learned the chicks were not to play with, the hens tolerated them around.

We are stuffing hay into the barn loft as fast as it dries. I am so afraid it will get rained on as our rainy season is due, soon. Actually, it was due to start a week or so ago. But the garden is certainly producing beyond expectations because it is late. Even my corn has ears forming. Usually they are miniature corn and I can them whole to add to Chinese stir fry. This year, they may mature. I would like to dry and save some seed from them if so. It looks like some of the winter squash I planted may even mature. They are still good as immature squash but don't keep and I can't save seeds from them then.

Most of the seeds Dan brought back on the first trips to town were heirloom seeds so should grow true from saved seeds unless cross pollinated from nearby plants. Any I plan to save seeds from, I bag the flower as soon as it opens and pollinate true from the same type. Then I keep it covered until I know it is developing and mark the fruit to keep track of and save. It takes a bit of time, but is worth it. Rose is saving seed also, so we can share and exchange seeds to keep the strains stronger.

Amy has made a play for Noah. I knew I should have just shot her. But if he is weak enough to fall for that, then I probably don't want him anyway. I happen to overhear her talking to him behind the barn, while I am in the barn. Neither know I am there. She must be rubbing up against him as he tells her to get back, she is in the way. She is practically purring as she tries to insinuate herself into his space. He finally shoves her aside and flat tells her to either help or go home. She makes a crude suggestion and he tells her if he were not a gentleman, he would slap her sillier for even suggesting such a thing. Does she think he and I are just friends or related? No, we are married and he believes in his marriage vows besides being in love with his wife.

Wow, he doesn't mince words with her. She starts sniffling and he tells her to dry the crocodile tears and go find someone that will actually want her. Then she calls him a nasty name and I step out and deck her yet again.

This time I hit the side of her jaw and don't injure my hand as much. See? I do learn. Noah does even better, he rushes over and grabs my hand to make sure I didn't hurt myself. Then he swings me around and gives me one of his toe curling kisses. Al and Natalie walk up about then and they have seen it from me taking my swing to the kiss and just stand there looking at us.

Amy was supposed to be helping Natalie can vegetables from the garden today, but had taken off. Al was about to offer Dan enough of his precious gas for him to fly her somewhere a long ways away from us. Preferably where she couldn't join forces with others like her to come cause us problems later. We offered to throw in 5 gallons to the cause.

Al heads down the road and Natalie stays with us. By the time Amy is starting to come around, Al and Dan are back with the idling airplane. We carry out 5 gallons of gas, a bag of assorted dried fish and bear and load Amy into the plane. Noah rides along with Dan in case there is any trouble and so if he needs help, he has it. They fly south, and land just outside a small settlement. They offload Amy and the supplies we have given her and take off immediately.

On their way home, they pass over an overturned tractor trailer. They land and walk over to it. It was full of dry food stuffs. Flour, sugar and cornstarch, among other baking supplies.

No one has opened the doors, so they feel okay with taking all they can haul then close the doors and seal it back up so nothing spoils the rest of the load for anyone else finding it.

Again, Dan is hauling far more than the plane was designed for, but he did some modifications on it that increased the lift and power. He felt confident as long as he balanced the load and it could still get off the ground, that he could haul it. They made it home, so he must have been right. He stopped at each driveway and as folks heard the plane, they were out waiting to see why he was driving it down the road. They off loaded flour and sugar at each place. Plus a variety of the other items they found in the trailer. It must have all been bakery goods as there were spices and herbs in the load, also.

Al and Natalie were still at our place when Noah and Dan pulled up out front. They borrowed my garden cart to haul their share of the flour, sugar and salt that Al wanted, home. We used the wheelbarrow to haul ours to the house.   Dan went on home with his.

He said if that Amy gal could have got a personality transplant, he would have considered letting her stay at his place, but as soon as she started talking, he was willing to air drop her wherever they happened to be at the time.   After he mentioned that, she was quiet the rest of the trip.

Chapter 9

Winter was closing in fast and we still had quite a bit left to do.   We put a small wood stove in the greenhouse to see if we could extend the growing a bit longer. I placed the tomato plants in 5 gallon buckets on the sun porch. Lettuce was transplanted into flats and also on the sun porch. Some of the herbs were repotted and set on the sun porch with the lettuce. We gathered all the drying bagged vegetables we were wanting to take seeds from and placed them inside to continue drying. When we picked the corn, we were pleasantly surprised to find we had enough to can some and share a bit, besides seed to save for next year. We cleaned it and broke ears into cobettes as they used to call them in the stores. There would only be one per person, but it had been a while since anyone had any at all. This would be a small treat, I hoped. Home grown corn isn't a big deal anywhere but in Alaska. Up here, it is unusual to get a crop.

Snow held off a bit but we did get a frost, then another frost. The outdoor tanks and washer were all drained and put away. All the inside containers were full of water and stored for winter use. The goats had a nice winter coat growing and the little caribou was almost a big caribou now. I wondered if when she came in heat if we may have a bull show up from the small herd in the White Mountains. Most of the time she was in a small corral out by the barn. I think I will keep an eye out for one showing up. I would not want a caribou bull in rut, but it would be nice to raise some domestically. If she calved next spring, we would be on our way to raising some.

I kept her hobbled while in the corral, just in case she did have a visitor. Maybe I could catch her again if the fence got knocked down.

A week or so later, we heard a clatter outside and it was too dark to tell exactly what the problem was, but the goats and dogs did not raise the alarm as they do with bears. Sure enough, in the morning, she is standing near the barn, looking a bit ruffled but not injured or frightened. The fence is down along one panel, so we repair it and write the date on the calendar. Just in case.

Still the snow holds off. It must be making up for being so early last year. We continue stocking up on as much firewood as possible. It is easier to drag home now that the ground is frozen. The dogs seem to enjoy working in the cooler weather, also. The bugs being gone is the part I like best. By the time we quit at night, we collapse into bed and fall asleep instantly. Well, almost instantly.

Chapter 10

Back in Canada, Liz and her group are doing great. The cattle and horses are fattening up very well before extreme cold hits. The chickens are still laying and everyone has searched the area around for plants to harvest that volunteered after last year's quake and not being harvested. It is surprising how many garden areas and fields still have vegetables growing in them. The first frost did damage several varieties, but then it warmed up a bit and there were many more crops that were still able to be harvested.

They left some to scatter more seed for the next year in case anyone came by needing food. The wagons were restocked with bags of grain and the dried foods as they were bagged up. The wagons were pulled into a semi-collapsed barn that still had half standing and sturdy when it was checked out. The house was repaired enough to live in comfortably. Firewood, the never ending firewood gathering was a daily project for everyone. There were always a few people left at the house, not only to have a meal prepared when the wood cutters returned, but to keep an eye out for intruders or thieves.

So far, they had been lucky not to have crossed paths with any except the group while still in Oregon. There were enough of them now to discourage all but a large group and being very well armed helped a lot. Mary was supervising in the kitchen when Shirley yelled that someone was bothering the chickens. The youngsters all ran toward the chicken coop, screaming like banshees and brandishing weapons.   The person at the chicken coop took off running across the field but was tackled by fast moving young adults.   By the time they dragged him to his feet, he looked a lot worse for wear.   He was a young man, not any older than the ones that tackled him.   He was more embarrassed by being caught by mostly girls, since it was 2 girls that tackled him.   They marched him back to the house and sat him at the table. He was so hungry he was practically drooling from the delicious smells wafting through the kitchen.

Mary dished up a bowl of stew and handed it to him.   He burned his mouth but continued eating, like he was afraid she would take it back.   The rest of the group went back outside to finish up their chores.   Soon his stomach rebelled against the food, too much too soon.   He tried his best not to lose it, but soon rushed outside.   Mary brought him a towel and showed him the set up for washing up.   He was so embarrassed by wasting food, he apologized, then introduced himself as Leif.   Mary brought him a cup of broth which he sipped carefully.

She asked how he came to be out here alone and why he tried to "borrow" a chicken. He told her everyone he asked for help chased him away.   His family died in the quake and he was just trying to stay alive.   After he ate the cup of stew she handed him next, he offered to wash the dishes for her. That won her over to his side. The rest of the afternoon, she fed him small amounts of food and he helped in the kitchen, offering to do any chore she needed done.

When the wood cutting crew and the gathering crew returned in the evening, Mary pulled Liz and Richard aside and explained about the spare young man getting ready to eat with the group. They agreed to let him join them on a trial basis. That is, if he wanted to move north. If not, he could stay on here and probably make a go of it.

When they offered him the chance to go with them on a trial basis, he accepted. He didn't know anything about farming or ranching, he was a city kid out of his element but willing to learn.

They figured by spring when they started moving again, he would know a lot more about being self-sufficient.

In the days that followed, he was a willing pupil to anyone interested in showing him how to do things. Some of the younger ones tried to take advantage by getting him to do their chores, but that was nipped in the bud. He learned to ride and work with the horses. How to harness up the larger horses to pull a wagon of hay out through the fields to feed the cattle once the standing grass was gone. After the snow came and got too deep for the wagon, they made a sort of sleigh for the horses to pull hay on.

The tractor running on wood fascinated him. So he worked with Mike many hours learning how it worked and how to build another one for the old tractor they found in an outbuilding. This would increase how much they could haul along with them and help their chances of surviving.

One morning while the wood crew was out cutting wood, they saw someone walking along, staggering once in a while, dragging a small sled behind them. One of the group went down to see who it was and found a young woman pulling her small child on the sled. She had bags piled around the child and they were both very thin. Richard offered her part of his lunch and so did the rest of the crew. She sat down and ate with them, sharing everything with the wide eyed silent child.

They asked how she happened to be out here alone and she said her husband died a while back from an injury and then infection and no medical help. She and her daughter were trying to find someone to join up with. Richard offered to let her come back to the house with the crew later that day, and see if she wanted to stay a while or how it worked out. She thanked him and accepted.

She and the child walked around a bit off and on to keep warm, and when the crew headed back, pulling their loads of wood, she offered to help. They thanked her and said she had enough load pulling the child and her belongings on the sled.

She stood waiting while the wood was stacked and came in the house behind the rest of the crew. The child never uttered a sound, just watched everything carefully. She was probably around 2 years old, maybe a bit older, but so quiet and solemn she seemed much older.

The woman introduced herself as Sara and her daughter, Tina. Richard took her over to talk to Liz and they talked while dinner was being placed on the table. Everyone was soon gathered around the table and heads bowed in prayer for the food and good day. Then everyone started serving themselves and laughing and talking. Sara relaxed and slowly ate her food and made sure her daughter had small amounts to eat, but not too much at once. She had been on short rations long enough to know they would get ill if they overate.

Beds were moved around in the large room the girls all shared, and another bed made for Sara and Tina. Some sheets were hung between beds for a small measure of privacy, and the girls moved them around some to give Sara the same courtesy.

When Sara and Tina came downstairs the next morning, they were dressed to go outside. Liz asked them what they wanted to do today and she thought they should go help bring in firewood.   Liz asked her if she could do mending or if she minded doing it and Sara brightened immediately.   She loved to sew and enjoyed mending.

Soon she had Tina set up with some buttons and a large needle to make herself a necklace and she was seated with a pile of mending around her.   Everyone else went about their usual chores,

Liz and the younger girls were working on training a couple of the horses they had acquired on the way that looked large enough to pull the wagon.   They were starting to work together now on pulling and just needed more work before the trip north started again in early spring.   The girls wanted to drive wagon, so they were learning also.

Lori and Marsha were using the other team to feed cattle.   Rosi was working on a guy that had pulled some muscles yesterday lifting logs.

There was always a large pot of some type of soup or stew on the stove, for anyone needing lunch.   Sometimes it was lots of broth until they found more ingredients to add to it.

When Liz came in at noon and found Sara still mending and the pile around her less than half the size it had been, she told her she was not expected to ruin her eyes and her back, sitting there all day doing that.   She could just help out where needed, if she would. Sara said she did not want to be a burden and she didn't mind work. She would like to take Tina outside a bit and let her get some exercise. That would be fine, would she enjoy going to the chicken coop to check for eggs? The chickens were dropping off on production, but still getting a few every day.

After lunch, Sara and Tina went out to check for eggs and to see the chickens. After they came back in, Sara found Liz and told her that back down the road a ways, there was an old place that had a lot of turkeys running around in the woods. She couldn't catch any and didn't have a gun, so she just watched them. She said they roosted near the barn and if someone had nets, maybe they could catch some. She thought it was less than 5 miles, but wasn't sure. She drew a map and marked where she had seen most of the birds.

That evening at dinner, everyone wanted to go hunt turkeys. A change in diet would be good and if they could catch some unharmed, they could be kept in the coop with the chickens and would be a welcome addition to the flock.

After chores the next day, they rounded up as many nets and crates as they could find and went to do a scouting foray. When they came back, they had one turkey with them and plans for going before daylight the next morning to try catching the main flock unawares. They cleaned the turkey and it would be roasted for dinner tomorrow night.

Several wanted to be in on the catching, so a fairly large group left well before daylight the next morning. Liz followed with a wagon full of crates. It's going to be fast and frantic if they actually catch any with the nets.

From the sounds, most of the flock roosts inside the barn and the main doors are open. Ladders are taken off the wagon and used to string nets across the main doors. People with dip nets are at the open windows. As the sun starts over the horizon the flock awakens and starts out the doors. When they hit the net, pandemonium breaks loose. By the time the nets are folded and put back on the wagon, the crates are full of large angry birds. People have been pecked, birds have been crated and they are headed back.

There are many that were not caught, so maybe they will survive to become feral turkeys. They are already mean enough to be.

Unloading them was almost as much fun as loading them had been. Since they were not gentle birds, it was decided to leave them in the crates overnight and make a separate pen and coop for them the next day. As mean as they were, they might damage the chickens.

Dinner that night was a magnificent meal. The food was excellent and the turkey was done to golden brown perfection. Some pies had been made to finish it off and everyone sighed in contentment.

When the first turkeys were turned into their new pen the next morning, they tried flying over and hit the mesh roof. So the rest of the flock had feathers of one wing trimmed so they couldn't fly at all. Feed was put out and they settled in to eat. The water had to be changed frequently as it froze within a few hours of being placed in the pen.

At lunchtime, the soup was made from the remains of last night's turkey dinner and everyone managed to come get a bowl. Homemade noodles filled the rich broth and again, everyone was content with the change in diet.

Winter settled in and everyone settled into their routines for the duration.

Chapter 11

Back in Alaska, I was getting ready to pull my hair out. One of the girls that came out with Sam decided she wanted to learn knitting from me but she really didn't. She just wanted to get away from having to work over where she was staying. She didn't mind eating the food, using the library they had or keeping warm by their fires, but she didn't want to work to maintain it. Selfish and self-centered came to mind to describe her. As far as I was concerned, she could go join Amy.

Finally, I told her to quite wasting my time and stay home. She flounced out of the house and went home. Well, I thought she went home, but then later I found out she went down to pester Al and Natalie. They soon kicked her out so she went to Jeremy and Ashleys.

Somehow she don't get the hint and soon they are kicking her out, too, so it is on to Will and Shari's. Shari is smart and hands off the twins to her and goes visiting. It's the first break she has had since Ashley got married. She stays over at my place a couple of hours and we have a very good visit. By the time she gets home, Maggie was more than ready to go home and do some of the work she was supposed to be doing. Year old twins will do that to you.

As winter settled in, everyone relaxed a bit and maybe a bit too much. The guy that showed up from town direction figured we couldn't be too far out when the plane kept showing up. So he just kept walking out this direction. He seems okay, but now we are back on full alert. We do not have supplies to feed extra mouths showing up. He brought some food with him, but not enough for the winter. He did get right in and helped out on whatever needed done, so we allowed him to stay in the little cabin. Pal liked him, so that was a vote in his favor. The cats even like him.

While we were sitting around the table after dinner a few nights later, he suggested we start keeping a lookout posted. He said he was not the only one that noticed the plane and the direction it came from. He said there are a couple of groups still around town. One is evil and not above murdering everyone if they thought they could profit somehow from it. The other group isn't as bad, but they are not very nice people, either. Some of the members are probably good people, but the leaders are not. For safety, everyone has to join one of the groups and the leaders run them with an iron fist. There are punishments for not following orders or the leaders' rules. Both are run as quasi-military units without the better qualities.

There aren't many of us here, to keep a watchman on duty all the time and where would someone do this? We really are not very defensible. Too spread out and too much cover any direction.

After we talk it over with the rest of the folks, it is decided to build a small heated cabin on an overlook bluff a ways down the hill from Dan's cabin. I have no idea how they think that is going to help us fight off interlopers. Maybe if they see we are expecting them, they won't bother us? I don't think so. Who knows how they will arrive, anyway? Are they going to try ATVs or snow machines and if so, they must have a better supply of fuel than the guys found on their jaunts to town. They thought they had pretty much used all available gas. If nothing else, we are back on being more alert again. This fellow says his name is Joe, but gives no last name. It probably would not mean anything to any of us anyway.

Two of the hens are not laying and also never got broody, so I decide we will just use them instead of turkey this year as Thanksgiving dinner. Joe cuts their heads off for me and I pluck, singe and gut them, then we take them over to Rose. When we show up with the hens, she is happy to have Thanksgiving dinner decided on. She was planning on baking one of the smoked bear hams, but just didn't really want to have ham Thanksgiving and Christmas. I ask what we can bring and she says she has everything else, between her and Kara. If I want to bring some extra pies, that would be fine. Chocolate and coconut cream sound really good to me, she will make pumpkin from ingredients she has on hand yet. She still has some olives and cranberry sauce. I included a box of eggs in the bag with the chickens, so there could be deviled eggs made with powdered sour cream. She was getting an egg once in a while from her 2 hens and had saved them for the holidays, but getting the extra, she now had more to work with.

We walked over early enough on Thanksgiving to help with any last minute work needing done and to visit a bit. Dinner was early afternoon so everyone could get home before full dark. The days were getting fairly short now and no one wanted to be out too long and let the fire go out at home. We left shortly after dinner so we could get our chores done. Goats wait for no one when they need milked.

Now that we had 2 goats to milk, we had to make sure we had time morning and evening to take care of them. We were keeping a low fire going in the barn to keep them comfortable, also. The LED lights were wonderful for working in the barn now. The cheese making was coming along. We had some rounds aging that we had great hopes for, but we did make pretty good mozzarella. It wasn't the Italian type, but it melted on a pizza and tasted pretty good. I made some cottage cheese that wasn't bad, either. It was good in lasagna, too.

Butter was harder to do, since it requires about 5 gallons of milk to make one pound of butter from goats milk. The cream doesn't rise, so unless a person has a separator, which I didn't, 5 gallons has to be churned to get the butter. Some of the buttermilk is needed for the cheese making, some I use in baking and the chickens get the rest. The chickens were handy for new experiments in cooking that went wrong.

Chapter 12

A couple of weeks before Christmas, we had our first extreme cold spell of the winter. Luckily for us, that is when the attack if you can call it that came from town. It was probably fine when they started out and as the temperature dropped, instead of going back, they just kept coming.   By the time they stumbled onto Dan's cabin, they just wanted someone to rescue them.   If they had asked nicely, he might have let them come in, but banging on someone's door when you are freezing to death and demanding that they help you isn't the way to do it.   Part of the band had stopped and built a fire, but they were under an evergreen and the snow came off the tree onto the fire and the ones too close.   Then they couldn't get another fire going.   The guys that had been so tough and feared in town, were not that much good out in the boonies.   From the initial group of 10, there were 6 by the time they reached Dan's.

The girl, Melanie, that had been coming to see Dan ever so often, since he moved here, walked up about the time they demanded he let them in and one man grabbed her, thinking hostage.   He may have been stronger, but not by much.   She had been cutting firewood and carrying it all summer and was in excellent condition and she was not cold.   She punched him in his red swollen cold nose and put him to his knees.   Then she smacked both his ears and put him on the ground.   Then she walked past the silent men and into the house.

The blood from his nose was freezing on his face and he could not make his legs stand him back up straight.   His ears hurt and his nose was beyond simple hurting into agony.

Finally Dan relented enough to let them go into his little shed. He made them leave all weapons on the ground and held a gun on them while Melanie frisked them. Then she went into the shed and started the small wood heater going. After she came back out, the men filed in and Dan shut and locked the door. Several objected, but not too strenuously as they didn't want forced back out into the cold. Melanie picked up the weapons and brought them into the cabin. There was a pretty good assortment. Guns, knives and one hatchet.

By morning, the men locked in the shed were warm and back to being bad guys in their minds. While Dan unlocked the shed, Melanie held one of their own rifles on them. When one lunged at Dan, she shot him through the thigh. The rest stopped and settled down. The wound did not hit bone and was really a small flesh wound, but the shock of being hit took all the starch out of the man. Then being forced to walk on his throbbing bleeding leg on up the road to Rose and Kara's added insult to injury. Melanie ran up to let Will and Shari know and then did the same at Jeremy and Ashley's. Dan kept them walking and made them stand outside while Melanie went in to get Kara. Kara was of the opinion they should just be shot, but not in her yard. They would smell and draw flies in the spring and maybe bears. When they asked Rose, she agreed with Kara. If asked, I would have agreed, also. These people were going to kill us. Now was not the time to be gentle with them.

Joe said these were none he was familiar with, so that left others out there willing to kill for our food.

Will and Jeremy showed up right after Kara and Rose gave their opinions and they voted with them. Jeremy offered to take them off Dan's hands and deal with the problem. Jeremy walks them back toward town. In the spring during breakup, some items of clothing were found along the river near the boat. No one asks.

We plan a small Christmas celebration for the day before Christmas, folks drop by during the day to visit and we exchange small gifts. Each family will be at home for Christmas day. I think this year, more than last, everyone is realizing just how much we are going to have to depend on ourselves and our neighbors just to survive. What Dan brought out by plane and Jeremy and Jim brought by boat will probably be the last manufactured items any of us will ever have to use. It is a solemn day but also a joyful day of thanks for the birth of the Christ child and what it means to us.

After Christmas, we try to stay alert to outside dangers, but it is hard to be alert every minute of every day.

During the gold rush mining days, there was a small community north of us. Then, in the 1980's, BLM decided the town was illegally platted and burned the entire town to the ground. The town still shows on maps, but all that was there, was a DOT station for road maintenance. In the hills north of the old town site, a few hardy souls still had their homes, located on patented claims or small lots sold by the State at later dates. I often wondered how the folks were faring out there, but it was over 20 miles and a bit far for a day's hike just to possibly get shot at for trespassing. Most of the folks there took their privacy very seriously. Noah had stopped by a few while employed to survey folks in the area, and no one would speak, and several threatened bodily harm if he didn't leave. So he left and marked them uncommunicative on the survey.

So we were very surprised a few days after Christmas when a dog team pulled into our yard. Al and Natalie had sent them on here, as they could not assist very well. The fellow's wife was in labor, and on the sled. When we got her in the house and on a mattress on the floor near the heater, she was in the final stages, but not progressing and not comfortable. Noah went out to do chores so she would have more privacy, and her husband and I checked things out. The baby had one arm turned wrong and was not able to proceed. Since my hands were smaller than his, I scrubbed up as well as possible and then used some olive oil on my hand and between contractions, managed to push the baby back enough to straighten out the arm while her husband held her down and kept me from getting hit often. Once the arm was pushed in the right position, everything happened very fast and she had a very upset and squalling infant on her tummy. I checked the baby's arm and it was not broken from my turning it. The cord was cut and tied. We waited for the afterbirth and checked it to make sure none had stayed inside. She wanted to go home immediately, but I talked her into staying at least overnight to make sure she didn't have any complications although how I would have dealt with any, I haven't a clue. This was my first human birth. Puppies, kittens and a couple of calves were the extent of my expertise.

Her husband and I cleaned up the mess and got her settled comfortably on the couch. Noah finally came back in and we all introduced ourselves. The man, Steve, looked hard at Noah and said, "You're that government guy."

I busted up laughing since that was what I had called him when I first met him also. Noah grinned sheepishly and admitted he did have a short term job for the government just to take that survey. He once thought it would be a good way to meet folks in the area and decide where he wanted to settle down. Steve's wife was Dani.

They had not decided on a name for the baby. They had been positive it would be a girl and they had a healthy little boy. He said they could call it Boy 1, she said if he thought he was going to have Boy 2 any time soon, he better think again. She had the first one, he could have the second and she would take over from there. He grinned at her and she grinned back, I think there will be a Boy 2.

I dipped out some soup from the pot on the stove and she sipped from the mug. Steve's stomach rumbled about then and I realized we all could probably use something to eat. It took longer to deliver a baby than I thought and all that had to be done after.

Noah finished up the chores and Steve helped pack in firewood. They were excited to see chickens and learn of the goats. They wanted to know if they could make a deal with us for a couple of chickens and maybe later, a goat or at least some cheese and milk.

I had been filling washed out water and soda bottles with extra milk and freezing them on the porch, so when they left the next morning, I sent eggs, frozen milk, smoked salmon, a smoked bear ham hock and some cheese with them. She told me the gifts were worth having to give birth just to meet us. She was one that took my road signs seriously back when she drove by once in a while and knowing how they felt about people just stopping in, she understood and did not stop to introduce herself earlier.

After they were gone, Noah and I relaxed a while in front of the fire. They seemed like they would be nice neighbors but actually lived too far away to visit often.

About a month later, they were back. She didn't produce enough milk for Boy 1 and the goat's milk we sent was all that he was able to keep down. They were frantic. The bottles they went home with were brought back sparkling clean and they wondered what they could trade for goat's milk. He had brought some lovely furs and moose hides they had tanned last winter and earlier this winter. I would have given them milk for the boy but they would not accept that. I poured the milk I had cooling from the mornings' milking into the cleaned bottles and we added more from the porch. She would have enough now to last through the rest of the winter, but if they ran low, come back over. Boy 1 was growing and filling out to be an adorable little guy. He slept most of the time they were there, but when he did wake up, he blinked and smiled at everyone. She said he did that on purpose. Daytime was his favorite time to sleep and nights were another story.

As usual, I had a pot of soup on the wood

stove, so we invited them to join us for lunch before they had to head home.   It was going to be a long day for them and their dogs and they snacked the dogs before coming in to eat.

When they left, I sent more eggs and cheese with them, as we were making quite a bit of cheese and with the LED lights on in the morning to extend light for the chickens, they were laying better this winter.

We were delivering eggs and milk to the other households also.   Will and Shari used quite a bit of milk for their twins.   Their chickens were laying enough eggs they didn't need extra as they used them sparingly.   Dan wouldn't touch the milk, but did like some eggs once in a while, the same with Jeremy and Ashley.   All enjoyed the cheese though.

We definitely got our exercise hiking around delivering milk, eggs and cheese.   But we also managed to keep in touch this way and make sure everyone was doing okay. Dan and Melanie were planning on getting married sometime this spring.   They had not set a date yet.   Dan was used to being completely alone on his trapline on the Porcupine, but was fast getting accustomed to living as part of a small community.   Maybe it was because no one bothered him very often and he could always say no to visitors and no one took offense.

Roman was working on some ideas he had

for tools to help on haying and grain gathering. Thad was spending a lot of time down at Kara's. She didn't seem to mind and said he had sense enough not to be underfoot all the time and gave her space. She might even let him stay. They both enjoyed reading and she had about as many books as her mother did.

Rose and Roman worked well together, enjoyed each other's company and she was helping him with his designs on his tools. She also had a very large library of books and usually there was something, somewhere, if they just looked hard enough, that helped out.

The books about making wood gasification plants were of interest but he was not sure any of their vehicles were old enough to have it work on them, so was going to try making one for a generator system for electricity.

Kevin was training everyone in martial arts, and all the girls were taking the classes also. They really wanted to know how to protect themselves since the group that came just before Christmas. Melanie was lucky she got in a good punch to the nose on the man, but if not, the results may have ended far worse for her. So she wanted to know all the moves and pressure points. Even the small boys were learning to protect themselves and everyone was now comfortable with their handguns and rifles. Jeremy helped once in a while and he had other skills to teach us all.

By spring, we should all be better prepared to defend ourselves from harm, with or without weapons.

We now had 2 more baby goats, a female and a male. I was busy making cheese and we spent more time milking. The 2 month break from milking hadn't given us a break as the other nanny gave birth just before the break. This gave us 4 females and 2 males. It was time to find out who else wanted to have goats. We would need to keep them until summer, as they needed a barn and to plan on hay enough to feed them.

Will and Shari wanted to start raising goats also. So they would be the first ones to get a pair. They had room to grow hay already cleared. They had outbuildings they may be able to convert over to a barn with hay storage. They needed to build some good strong goat proof fences though.

Our caribou was showing signs of increasing the caribou population, also. She looked like it may be twins. Usually a first calf is a single calf, but she had a pretty good diet and not much stress in her life, so maybe she would produce twins her first try.   I was glad Al brought her to me as a new calf.

I wasn't sure what we were going to do with caribou, but they made good meat if butchered before rut. They could pull a pretty good load, also. So we just kept working with her. She was not too good about going exactly where we wanted, so usually had to be led. But she did not mind the harness or pulling the load.

The seeds saved from last harvest were picked through and a few started for the next crops.

Everyone was sick of the same foods so we butchered several of the roosters and cut them up and shared them out. We should have done it earlier in the winter and just froze the meat until needed. It would have saved us feeding out a lot of chicken food although they did get our table scraps and only some additional grains. The wild grass seed seemed to work well for them. Since Roman made the small mill that removed the beards from the foxtail grass seeds, we were able to use those, also. The animals all ate them and without the beards, they were not a danger to the animals.

Roman and Rose also made alcohol from the wild grains in a still they set up. Then she used it to make tinctures for medicines. She made a lingonberry liqueur that was a marvelous cough syrup and helped with flu, also. She was pretty good at spotting fake coughs.

She had bags of dried plants she gathered in the summer and prepared. She kept them labeled as some are dangerous if consumed. Each has its place as a medicine, but it has to be handled and used carefully. She kept at me to learn more of the uses of the plants. I did learn many of them.

The shrubs that looked so nice at her driveway, were actually baneberries and deadly poison. She said you never knew when that may come in handy to know. Each household had a small jar of the dried berries labeled and put back on a top shelf. Same with some of the mushrooms that grew in summer.

We were all working on our early spring projects, just waiting for the snow to melt and ground to thaw so we could plant. Noah started the small wood stove in the greenhouse to warm it up faster. Then he dug out the planting beds and shoveled in goat and chicken fertilizer and replaced the soil. We started some seeds out there to transplant out into the garden later and some to keep in the greenhouse. The fresh fertilizer under the soil would heat the soil and maybe keep the whole greenhouse warmer.

Chapter 13

We didn't even get into the next fight that
occurred. Well, we didn't in the first either,
such as it was. But the second attack really
was an attack. Dan heard them coming and
fired a couple of shots to get Will and
Jeremy's attention. They came with guns and
so did Ashley. Shari had the twins and
couldn't help, but set up in her upstairs

window with one of the large rifles with a good scope.

The snow machines came up out of the valley with guns out and started firing random shots into Dan's cabin.   Dan was on the other side in a shelter he built after the last group came by.   Jeremy was above them behind some well-placed logs and Ashley was over on the other side, also behind some logs.   As the attackers fired on the cabin, the defenders opened fire from all sides down into them. Shari did her part from the hill and picked off the apparent leader that was staying over to one side directing the attack.   She had spotted him by watching where the attackers kept looking to the side. Once he was gone, the attackers lost heart, but it was a bit too late and everyone kept firing until they were all down.

They stripped off all usable clothing to wash, patch and save then took the bodies back to the river and chopped a hole to throw them through.   Might as well feed fishes.

Joe, Thad and Melanie showed up in time to help on cleanup and Joe identified the leader as one of the ones he warned about, earlier, Tom Taylor.   He said he ruled his group through fear and punishment and the world was better off without him.

Dan was angry, they broke one of his windows in his cabin.   Windows were not something easily found.   Will gave him one from the salvage pile they started just after moving here when they found out how much was discarded at the Transfer Sites around Fairbanks. They soon had the broken window out and the new one in place.

By backtracking, the place the attackers camped the night before was found and the sleds they stashed there contained extra ammo, more fuel and oil and winter camping gear. All was salvaged and could be used. Then the snow machines were stored out in the woods near the outbuildings. There was not much to be used from them at present.

Everyone was a bit shaken by the killing. But after the rest of us thanked them and congratulated them enough, they got over most of the feeling sick about it. Shari had not been sure she could actually pull the trigger on a human, but as she saw what they were doing and how her babies would fare if they won, she had no trouble becoming a sniper. Ashley was worried for Jeremy and the guys both knew how the women would fare and the babies if they lost, so everyone was motivated to be the survivors. This was no time to let anyone get away. They could bring back more and maybe the next attack would be sneakier and they would succeed.

The men and most of the women started making it harder for anyone to sneak in from the direction of town. They started on each side of the old roadbed and fell trees leaning

them into other trees and making a real
jumble across the whole lower valley. Then
they dragged more trees across the road,
building a barricade. Anyone trying to get
through or around would need to do some
clearing if they were motorized and just be
difficult on foot.

Then they came a bit farther up the road
and did the same thing again. Leaving a
series of trees down, trees hanging in other
trees and trees across the road. Maybe it
would be enough to give some early warning
of intruders. It was going to take some work
to get through those.

Then, since that seemed like a good idea,
they did the same thing as a fence of sorts
around each property. They spent several
weeks working on this and it did give a bit
more sense of security even if maybe a false
one. Around the properties, they added small
poles across gaps in the "fence". When we
did ours, we made it into a real fence so we
could let the caribou cow out to graze and she
seemed to appreciate it. She was not
extremely tame and I worried she would find
a way out and we would never see her again.
However, when it was time for her to calve,
she came to the barn. She gave birth to twins
and they were adorable little calves. Almost
black and so very fast as soon as they were on
their feet. We immediately caught and haltered
them, to get them used to humans right away.

She seemed content to let us handle the calves and stayed at the barn without trying to escape. About a week after the calves were born, a wolf came into the yard and we shot him. After that, she was more inclined to feed farther from the barn, but we kept the calves in a corral and she came back for their feedings every few hours.

We kept on training the calves and goats to pack and be led. Yes, we had dogs, but extra pack animals of any sort may come in handy at some point and rather have them willing from the start than trying to force them when we needed them most.

The early rows were planted in the garden and small green shoots were showing under the plastic cover. I don't know how we will manage once all the plastic is too brittle to use. We carefully fold ours up and keep it in the barn in a dark corner to keep sunlight off it. We have several unopened rolls also kept in the dark under cover, so are good to go for many years yet. Still, thinking of the future worries me some.

With 2 of the goats gone, the chores don't take quite as long. We still have a lot of hay left over from last year and that gives us a bit of leeway on how much we absolutely have to cut for the coming winter. Here the snow isn't even off the ground and I am thinking about next winter.

I'm turning into a worrywart. I have a

sneaking hunch I may be pregnant and at the moment, am not too happy about it. With any luck it is early menopause. I am too old to start raising a family now. I am set in my ways and don't have a maternal bone in my body. I have no idea how Noah is going to react to this news. We never talked about having a family, maybe we both thought that was behind us. What if it is born handicapped because of my age? I am in my early 40's and not exactly mommy material. Maybe I can slip it into the goat pen and let one of the nanny's raise it until it is old enough to be housebroken. Nah, someone would notice.

By the time I decide maybe I am pregnant or else I have a very active internal growth, Noah hesitantly asks me if I am okay. I have been grouchy and moody for a couple of months now, and he has more than noticed. To my surprise and his, I burst into tears. That makes me mad which makes me bawl harder. Poor Noah doesn't know what to do and that makes two of us. So I plop on the ground and just let the tears flow as if I could stop them anyway. Noah kneels down beside me and gathers me into his arms and just holds me, which seems to be exactly what I needed. Slowly I stop with the crying, I hate a crying female and to be one is worse yet.

"Noah, what would you think of becoming a father?"

Suddenly he is sitting on his butt on the ground right beside me. His face has gone white and I am afraid he might pass out. I figured he would be surprised, but this is worse than I expected.

Then he grabs me in a hug that almost squeezes the breath out of me. "A child? We are going to have a child?"

He is so excited he wants to run over and tell his Dad immediately. I have to let him know I could be mistaken and it may be a false alarm or I may not be able to carry to term. I would rather wait to tell anyone until it is a sure thing. But he walks around the rest of the day with a goofy grin on his face and whistling as he works. Well, I guess he isn't upset. I probably shouldn't tell him I considered letting the goats raise it.

He tries to do all the chores and starts treating me like I am made of glass. Oh heck no, this isn't the way we are going to do this. I'm pregnant, not sick, so we have a talk and go back to doing things the way we did before, although I do step back and let him do the heavier lifting.

We are in the middle of cutting next winter's firewood and Noah keeps trying to make sure I don't overdo it. Finally I tell him I won't overdo, we just need to get the wood done. I am used to this work and it isn't going to hurt me. If I tried dragging a whole tree up the hill, then maybe it might. So we settle back into our routine and get the woodshed filled.

We start another pile beside the barn for use in the small stove there. Then we put a bit of roof over it to protect it from getting buried under snow. When we have nothing else to do, we cut more firewood. Then we start cutting hay. We might be a bit early on the hay, but want to get it in while the weather stays warm and dry.

Soon, the guys are planning on the fish harvest with the boats. Al is the one that knows more about that, so several of the guys hike to Al's to see what he wants to do this summer. They decide to hike down and climb over the log piles in the next few days and take out the boat and check on salmon run. When they get back, they are excited and have a couple of large King or Chinook Salmon they managed to dipnet from the boat. They quickly grab some of the folded nets and head back out and by evening, we are inundated with salmon. These are the large fat fish everyone wants to find in their nets and usually not used as dog food. So we clean fish and prepare to smoke these for human consumption.

We have been building drying racks to dry salmon for the dogs, but will have to wait for those. They should be along in a few days and we were lucky to be in the right place to catch these. Every household but Kara's will have a large bag of squaw candy from this. That is the long thin strips, rich and tasty and very good trail food. Very high in calories, too.

The next day when they come back in at noon, they already have the boat full to the point of danger. About half are more Kings and the rest are Silvers also known as Coho salmon. So some are cleaned for strips and the folks that want some fresh salmon and the others are filleted, tails left on and cut across to the skin, and hung over the poles to dry. The cut strips of flesh hang out from the skin and dry quite well. Small smudge fires underneath help keep flies away. We constructed a quick pole shed to cover the drying racks and covered it with old tarps. It wasn't weather proof, but helps keep the smoke inside to keep bugs out. This can be used for dogs or humans. The heads and guts were again saved and buried for fertilizer.

We had more people and more dogs now, so we kept right on netting and drying as long as the run continued. After all the fish was dry, we disassembled the shed and racks and stored them high up the bank above high water mark for spring breakup. We might try again in August for Dog or Chum salmon. If the run is good for them, we will dry enough just for all the dogs and store the extra Silvers we have now. It is not always a sure run and we didn't want to wait and see whether there were going to be enough for the dogs.

This time, we didn't get the bears down along the river, just one at Rose's place. She had it curing and ready to smoke by the time the fish were done. Then she cleaned the smokehouse and started the bear. The hides are not prime in the middle of the summer but there will always be a use for them anyway, so it was curing, also. Work boots or mitts could be made from the finished hide.

We were all harvesting and drying hay and grain heads as fast as we could.

We picked up some old steel barrels we found over the bank along the road between us and Al's, and carefully cut the top off, then made wooden top cover and lined it with some newspaper plate metal. When the grain was dry, we filled the barrels after placing large trash bags in the barrels first. I had no idea what used to be in the barrels. They didn't smell or have any visible residue, but I didn't want to poison my birds and animals.

Toilet paper was a thing of the past. So I went to the rag bag and found all the old T shirts and trimmed them up to make personal clothes. I saved the body sections and used the sleeves for the personal clothes. We kept a spray bottle in the outhouse in the summer and sprayed, then used the clothes and placed in a container to be washed. We each had a container and each did their own wash. In winter, if we used the outhouse, we had to carry the spray bottle out to keep it from freezing, but usually used the indoor honey bucket and dumped it daily. Melted snow kept it rinsed and clean.

I felt like I was as big as a house by late summer. I guess I wasn't as big as I felt, but if my calculations were correct, it was due in late September. I used the rag bag again and made diapers from the T-shirt bodies and small sleepers from old sweats. There wasn't going to be a lot of variety in the layette. I had safety pins or duct tape and opted for the pins. Later, I would make some fur bunting and bags to keep it in.

Shari offered me some tiny disposable diapers she had left over from her twins. Plus most of the little clothes she had for them that they had outgrown. I had a feeling these little clothes were going to see a lot of use in the years to come and would take very good care of them.

I picked and dried a lot of moss to use as liners in the T shirt diapers. It is absorbent when dry and actually prevents diaper rash.

Noah loved to feel the baby moving around. He had a nice singing voice and would sing to the baby in the evenings. I told him he was setting a precedent there and the baby would expect that, later. He built a lovely small rocking bassinet. His Dad built a large crib. He even cut down a twin bed mattress and resewed the end to look like the

rest and delivered it one afternoon.   He
carried part, Thad carried the rest.

Roman was thrilled to finally be a
Grandpa.   He never thought it would
happen.   He walked over to check on me
every couple of days.   Sometimes Rose
walked over with him.   They always got in
and helped on whatever we were doing and
we visited while we worked.   Rose made me a
couple of blankets for the baby from some
fleece material she had on hand.   She said it
wasn't the usual baby colors, but it was warm.
One was a tied blanket, camo on one side and
hunter orange on the other.   One was black
on one side and purple on the other.   Well,
the baby would certainly not be bothered by
the colors and she was right, they were warm
blankets.   She suggesting leaving one end
untied and uncut to tie, until the baby was
larger, to use them as a sleeping bag while it
was little.   Then it could be cut and tied.

Chapter 14

In Canada, Liz and her group started getting ready to head north as the snow melted. Wagons were packed and unpacked only to repack. Several farm tools they found and made over the winter were included in the loads and never left the wagons, they were not negotiable.

There was a herd of elk that came in to feed with the cattle once in a while. A few of them had stayed as dinner throughout the winter.

There had been a couple of small squirmishes with some marauders intent on stealing from them. They suffered a few nicks and a graze or two, but nothing serious or even requiring stitches. They also helped out a few folks that came by needing help and willing to trade or work for what they got. They traded some of the cattle for assorted items folks had to trade. They kept most of the horses. They had turkey quite often for dinner and it was no longer such a treat.

A nice young couple settled on the farm a couple of hills over from them, and they gave them some chickens and turkeys. One cow they had was due to calve and did not look in good enough condition to travel, so they left her with the couple, also. They offered to let them just move into the place they were using, but the couple declined, it was too big for 2 people to work and they didn't want to take on more than they could handle. They did want to graft some of the trees to seedlings they found in their orchard. It was a small orchard, but not over mature and should produce well for them with some care. Liz showed them how to prune the trees and also pruned the ones they had used.

They were leaving the place in far better condition than they had found it. The roofs were repaired, the woodshed had a few cord of wood in it. The house and barns were cleaned.

They decided to leave after Sabbath on a lovely sunny day. The grass was growing enough for the cattle and horses to graze as they moved along. About a mile from the start, they met a wagon pulled by lovely draft horses, heading the way they had just came.

Liz and Richard stopped to talk to the family in the wagon. They were searching for some of their family that used to farm out this way. Their farm was destroyed and they wanted to settle farther inland.

No one knew for sure whether their winter home was the place these folks were looking for, but they told them about it and the turkeys over the way and still some chickens in the woods behind the house. They gave them a cow due to calf soon and wished them success on the place. They also told them about the young couple that just moved in and suggested they get acquainted. They could help each other out.

The first few days, they moved the herd slowly so they and the herd could get used to travel again. When they passed a small community, they traded some cows for some clothing that they could use and a few blankets. It wasn't a town, but may become one in the future. It was the largest community they had passed since leaving Oregon.

The people seemed nice and truly glad to

get some cattle.   The whole group only had 2 shotguns with half a box of shells, so they couldn't even really hunt for meat.   After talking it over, Richard shot a steer that seemed inclined to wander often.   They saved part for themselves and gave the rest to the small group.

Going up the Cassiar highway seemed the best route to take.   No really high mountain passes. No huge rivers to cross.   There were rivers, just not as big and worrisome as the ones on the Alaska Highway route.   They could not depend on the bridges being safe. Their first river crossing was made before the ice went out, so they crossed carefully and safely over the ice.   The smaller rivers and streams were already flowing, so they had to find safe crossings but it went fairly well. The routine came back to them as they went along and the new additions to the crew were good help. Sara helped wherever she saw anything needing done and willing to do whatever was asked.   Sara's daughter, Tina, still did not talk, but she smiled once in a while and did what was asked.   She was intelligent, just not wanting to talk.   She had started humming as she played by herself. Leif was willing to work at anything needing done.   Both were glad to be included on this journey and didn't mind moving to Alaska. They both appreciated regular meals.

The trip up the Cassiar went smoother and

faster than they expected. The weather was fine and enough graze along the roadway to keep the animals moving slowly but steadily all day long. Richard, Leif and Mike designed and build a cooker to use the heat from the wood gasifier on one of the tractors to cook a large pot of stew or beans as they traveled. Now they didn't have to stop early enough to cook a meal. The second cooker was more of an oven, and was attached to the other gasifier. So they could make some sort of bread, or roast meat as they traveled and add potatoes at a stop, for the evening meal. The smells drifting along as they traveled should have warned them that someone would show up hungry and wanting fed. It did happen a few times and they usually had enough to share some food. They picked up another couple of workers this way.

The new couple had some supplies of their own and he had some tools he wanted to bring along. So Mike went back with him on horses to load up. The shack they were living in wasn't much, but it was clean. The tools were a gunsmith's tools. If he had the materials, he could actually make guns.

His wife, Lela, sang beautifully and in the camps, she, Rosi and Marsha sang into the evenings.

Lela and Jeff married just before the earthquake and used to live near Smithers, B.C. They were traveling from Whitehorse when the quake hit and ran out of gas near where their shack was. They had a hard time since then. There were fish in the stream and they fished every day, drying extra that they caught, they set snares and ate rabbits. They were not sure on most of the wild greens and berries except the blueberries. They dried any extra and rationed themselves.

They were so thrilled to have vegetables back in their diet and enough food at any meal, they would be willing to move to Alaska or Timbuktu.

The cattle were paying the way north and still would have plenty when they got there. Since no one knew they were coming, they knew there would not be hay cut for winter or grain of any sort for the animals so they had to plan the trip to winter where there was hay. They figured if they could make it to Haines Junction area this season, they should be able to winter there as it had been a farming community.

When they passed the Whitehorse area, there was a small smoke as from a chimney across the river on the other side of the valley, but that was all the sign of anyone living there, that was seen.

Going around Kluane Lake was hair raising. Small and not so small slides along the lake side blocked progress and they had to clear it away in some spots to proceed with the wagons and tractors. The one tractor had a bucket on the front, so they could use it for part of the roadwork. But they had to be careful and not start another slide as they cleared a path just wide enough for the wagons. It took a little longer than planned to get by there, but they still reached Haines Junction area before winter set in.

It took some searching around before they found some old barns with hay in them. There was going to be a lot of fence repair needing done as fast as possible to keep the herd enclosed. The young adults all headed out with their tool belts and started restringing wire and nailing it back on fence posts. If they could get the top and middle done now, maybe the herd would stay on the good graze. The grass was chest high on the horses. There was a nice small stream running through the entire pasture area, so water for the herd would not be a problem. Finding a house to all live in might be a problem, but the herd was the main worry and that was solved. If nothing was found, they could always stay in the barns. What was found was a couple of houses that were collapsed. So after the herd was settled, most of the crew started salvage work.

One of the barns was near the large pasture and looked sturdier than the other 2. So they planned on using one of the barn walls as one of the house walls and build a house of sorts against the barn. They had a wood stove on one of the wagons, and could use it for heat in the place. They didn't have real insulation, so packed the walls with hay from in the barn. It may only last one winter before rodents ate it, but they only needed one winter.

The roof was salvaged metal sheets and some needed to be straightened quite a bit. They built a loft under the roof and filled it with hay for insulation also as the roof would lose heat badly. They found a couple of old scythes in the barn and cut the high standing grass and spread it on the floor inside. It wasn't fancy and if they found anything better, they would move into it later. Part of the barn was filled with baled hay, so they stacked bales and made sleeping quarters for most of the crew in the barn itself. The hay rooms were low ceilinged to hold in body warmth and boards placed across and more bales on top to make the room, then a tarp hung over the doorway. No matches allowed.

They would feed out of the other barns as long as possible to keep the sleeping rooms. Compared to sleeping outside as they had been doing most of the trip, it was pretty good accommodations.

Once a kitchen area was set up, and food supplies unloaded into the area, everyone concentrated on getting the outdoors work done. A crew immediately started on the firewood. Using the teams, whole logs were pulled into the yard for cutting into pieces for the stoves. One of the abandoned places they had passed a few days earlier, a lodge, supplied them with a propane cooking range and a very large tank of propane. The propane tank now rode in the front bucket on the tractor. Used carefully, it should last several years as it had been the fuel source at the lodge it was found at.

Liz found some fire bricks stacked inside one of the barns and brought several in to place on the heater stove. At night, each person could take a brick to wrap on a towel to warm their sleeping bags and feet. The house that used to be here near the barns was a burned shell and not worth trying to repair. However, later rummaging through the remains, several cast iron skillets and a large Dutch oven were found. Some heavy duty kitchen utensils were found and added to the supplies.

Everyone would need household implements once they reached the end of the trip, so now as some of the loads were used, they would pick up things to take as they found them or could trade for them.

There were elk in the area and a few deer, so they butchered some as needed to supplement their diet. Beef is fine, but it can't compare to a properly prepared elk steak. The hides were fleshed, stretched and work started on tanning them.

During the early winter, on one of the scouting forays, a small burned out town was discovered. At one end of the former town was a small fabric shop with most of the roof caved in and a lot of damage to it. Some of the roof was pulled aside and one person carefully picked their way into the wreckage of the building. She came out later with a huge bag of thread, needles and yarn. Then went back in and started handing out bolts of fabrics. Some had smoke damage on the outer layers, but a lot of each was still useable. She soon had a large pile of goods, so one of the crew went back for a wagon.

There was rodent damage to some of the material, but even those bolts were brought out. They could sort through and salvage in the warmth of the shelter during the winter. She found a couple of small hand crank repair sewing machines and added them to the pile. These were simple and usually considered children's learning toys, but they were still better than sewing everything by hand.

The best find was an old treadle sewing machine. It was under some of the collapsed roof and looked like it would need major work to make it good enough to use again. But, winter was coming and it could be a winter project.

They were pretty well set for their second winter on the trail.

Chapter 15

Back in Alaska, preparations for winter were coming along. Everyone had a good supply of firewood cut and stacked. Paul had a rocket mass heater in his home, so he only had to salvage the tops of the trees used for the other firewood. Jenna sat and cut the branches into the sized pieces needed to feed their stove and they had their woodshed stacked with what looked like a mad beaver dam on dry land. Their worse problem was the wild hares eating their wood and the occasional moose browsing in the woodshed. They finally had to enclose the shed to make it moose proof. They never figured out how to make it entirely bunny proof.

By the middle of September, I was not a nice person to be around. The baby had dropped and I thought I waddled. Harvesting the garden was a literal pain in the back, sides, belly, you name it.

I even went on a housecleaning frenzy. I hate cleaning house. Rose said it was my nesting instinct kicking in. I wanted to kick something alright.

Sure enough, one night after washing all the windows, when I relaxed to try to sleep, the small twinges I felt all day took over. Evidently that was the start of labor. I don't know about anyone else, but it felt like a bad case of food poisoning gone wrong. The only good part, I could relax between bouts. I woke up Noah when they got close enough together that there wasn't much break between them. By that time, I had an area prepared and a sheet of plastic under the sheet on the spare mattress on the floor. The water broke while I was on the honey bucket, so I wouldn't even have to clean that up.

While he was getting dressed, I plopped down on the mattress and proceeded to give birth. When the stream of cussing from the mattress got too loud, he came over to see what I was doing and I handed him our new child. "You were supposed to wait so I could get Rose to come over."

"Well, too late, give me a hand here, we need to cut the cord and stuff."

It was the "and stuff" that he really didn't want to get involved in. But being a nice guy, he did it anyway.

We got me cleaned up and the baby wrapped in a blanket and a little cap on its head to keep it warm. Neither one of us had looked to see whether we had a boy or a girl. When we realized that, we quickly unwrapped and found we had a little girl. Then one of us actually remembered to put a diaper on her. I was so glad Shari gave us those tiny disposables. Thinking of using a standard safety pin near that tiny body that felt so huge just a wee bit ago, scared me. Was duct tape such a bad idea?

Neither one of us had any experience with babies, especially tiny new ones. I never babysat anyone's kids when I was a teenager. Noah certainly didn't. Frankly, this little bundle of noise scared the pants off both of us.

Roman and Rose walked over later in the day and were surprised to meet the newest member of the community. We named her after Rose, Elaine Rose. Elaine was also Noah's Mom's name.

I nodded off partway through their visit, so I'm not sure when they went home. I woke up hearing sounds like a small kitten mewling. Well, at least she isn't screaming yet. I snuggle her up to me in my cocoon of covers and she nestles into my chest and falls right back asleep. Maybe this isn't going to be so bad.

The next time I wake up, it is to the sound of Noah softly singing and carrying our daughter while he starts breakfast. We have a chest snuggly carrier and he has her bundled into it so both hands are free to work. It gives her head full support and her eyes are watching his face intently.

I think he is going to be a good daddy. Maybe she won't have to be raised by the goats.

When she falls back asleep, he gently places her back in her bassinet. Then goes out to do outdoor chores. While he is out, I get dressed and tend the fire. Mornings are chilly and I'm afraid the baby will get chilled. Noah comes in just as I shove a large chunk of wood into the stove and almost has a fit. Something about just having given birth and should be resting. Like I wasn't aware I just popped out about 8 pounds of baby? Hey, I was there.

Then I realize he really is worried I might hurt myself and smile. He really is sweet and thoughtful. A warm comfy feeling of love settles over me and I let him baby me a while. I don't want to get too used to it, we have to get back to work in a while.

The French toast casserole he has baking in the oven brings us back to the present and he rushes to the kitchen muttering something about ruining breakfast. Sounds like me.

The next week really proves we love each other. The baby doesn't want to eat and when she does, she burps it right back up. She has lost weight and isn't thriving. We finally start giving her goats milk and she keeps it down. Oh great, she really does need to be raised by the goats. I was joking, honest.

As soon as she starts on the goat milk, she is good natured and seldom mewls. She still doesn't do the actual crying I associate with babies. I am not complaining.

Hmmm, maybe I found one small maternal bone deep in my body. This small person has changed the way I look at babies. She is sweet natured, which helps. I haul her around in the front carrier all the time, it is almost like being pregnant still but with a higher center of gravity. I'm glad most of the work getting ready for winter is done. She jerks a bit while sleeping when I am hammering, but nothing really bothers her too much. She does seem to expect to be sung to every night. Ha, told you so, Noah.

He doesn't mind a bit and sings to her as we prepare her for bed each evening. As he sings, she relaxes and soon is asleep. I think I fall more deeply in love with my husband just watching him with our daughter. Thanks to the goats, she is thriving at last.

Will and Shari are having a time with their two growing children. They are walking now and into everything. What one can't find to get into, the other one can.

Shari is using old clothes that are too warn to repair any more to make small pants and shirts for them. The lower legs of pants seldom actually wear out, so she cuts out a pair of small pants from the lower leg section of adult pants. She puts a drawstring waist on them. By making them quite large, they should last a while. Shirts are used the same way. Cut way down and resewn for little shirts for them. Both are dressed in pants and shirts as dresses aren't too practical. Small moccasins for their feet when they aren't barefoot.

She only makes 2 changes of clothes for each and washes them often, knowing she may never have more materials and old clothes to work with. She has become a most practical woman and a great shot. Certainly nothing much remains of the timid little mouse of a woman I met at first. Will is so enchanted by her that it is almost painful to see. He is as proud of each and everything she does that she smiles and playfully cuffs him. They are sweet together.

Dan and Melanie got married sometime

during the late summer when I was not paying attention. So I send over a late wedding present of cheese and eggs in a homemade basket. Noah delivers it and brings back many thanks and a box of nails Dan said were just taking up room in his storage shed. Yeah, right.

Al and Natalie come over to see how we are doing. They are really enjoying raising chickens now and gathered a lot of feed for them for winter. We reminded them to store a bucket of gravel too, for their digestion process. I saved the egg shells, dried, baked a bit and crushed them fine so they were not too familiar to the chickens then mixed in their feed to make sure their shells remained strong. I didn't want them to develop a taste for the shells, unbaked, and start pecking at their eggs.

Natalie said she would start doing that, she did save the shells but was adding them to the stuff for the garden bins.

They left after a short visit and said they were going over to see Rose about getting married. Not today, but soon. We wished them happy and said our goodbyes.

The first snow started that afternoon. It was lovely to look out the window and watch the flakes float lazily down. Even better was knowing our pantry and the ice house was fully stocked with food for us for the winter, the barn was filled with hay and grain for the animals and the animals were increasing enough to share with others.

I was back to making cheese and this winter we were going to practice on ice cream more. We made some last winter but not much and never had enough to share. This winter, we have a lot of berries in the ice house in small amounts of sugar preserving them. Maybe some birch syrup sweetening to see how that worked in the goat milk. The chickens might get even more experiments.

We were making block ice, by freezing water outdoors in 5 gallon buckets, then bringing the buckets in to thaw partly, just enough to tip the block of ice out, after pouring off the water to add to the next block. We were stacking the blocks in the ice house to use whenever we wanted to make ice cream or just wanted ice.

We left the inner insulated door open all winter and only closed the outer thin door to keep rodents or other creatures out of the building. Then when the weather started warming up, we closed the inner door. We could keep ice most of the summer this way.

Elaine kept growing and started getting more of a personality. She knew from the start if she smiled a certain way and batted her eyes at her Dad, she could wrap him around her fingers easily. It was a mutual admiration society and her Grampa was her willing slave. Her uncle was not far behind.

This girl had flirting skills before she could sit up that were better than mine had ever been. I watched in awe as she had 3 grown men all at her beck and call. Dang, she was good.

I think Roman and Thad would have moved in if we had more room. They walked over almost every day. Usually they had something for Elaine, and she crowed in delight when they came in the door. It was so entertaining to watch, I couldn't say they were spoiling her to death. She really didn't appear to be getting spoiled by the attention. She certainly is a loved little girl. I worried at first that the men would be disappointed in not having a boy to carry on the family name or whatever it is guys usually seem to expect from a little boy. They leave no doubt in my mind they are thrilled with a little girl. I don't think she will ever feel insecure in her "only being a girl".

I bundle her up and go visiting. I'm wanting to get out and walk and I think it would be good for both of us. She seems to enjoy being out and about in her cocoon.

We stop over and see Kara for a while. I love stopping here. She always has something interesting around and lots of books and movies. We enjoy a lot of the same books, and could talk for hours about them. This was one of those times.

I lost track of time and it is getting a bit toward dark when I head home. While walking, I hear footsteps behind me and when I walk, they walk, when I stop, they stop.   I really don't like this.   Then I almost step on a ptarmigan and about have a heart attack. The darn bird flies up right under my feet. It's a good thing the baby is firmly anchored in her cocoon, or I probably would have dropped her.   I was afraid to run, in case whatever was behind me might give chase.   I didn't scream because that wouldn't help either, but I did walk a bit faster and started talking to the baby to reassure her, I kept telling myself.   By the time I turn in our driveway, I am practically trotting, but still not running.   The footsteps behind me are keeping pace with me.   As I come over the rise toward the house, Noah is coming toward me with a rifle.   He yells drop and I do, keeping my arms out to protect the baby.   He shoots directly over my head and I hear a loud grunt behind me and I am up and over to the side, then running like I have never run before, around behind Noah.   He holds the rifle at the ready and we wait a few minutes. The large dark bump does not move.   We go in and get headlamps.   When we check the dark lump, it is a very large black bear.   Very fat and prime pelt.

We go back in the house and get the skinning and butchering supplies.   Then spread out the bear on its back and proceed to skin and dress it out.   There is enough fat on it to render several gallons of lard. We will definitely be making bacon from the rib meat. I will have to cut the slabs into quarters to fit them in the pans I cure the bacon in. This is one huge black bear. The meat smells okay, so it probably fattened on berries, no carrion or fish. The hams are very large, and the picnic hams are very large, also. This will be a prime addition to our larder.

We lug all the meat into the house and spread the hide in the yard, sprinkle it with some salt and roll it up. I started skinning up the head and feet before cutting them off to simplify finishing it tomorrow. We stash the hide in a box on the porch and start work on curing the pieces we brought in. Once all the pieces are in the cure out on the porch, we finally get to eat dinner. Neither of us know why the bear followed me. Curiosity or a late snack before hibernation, either one was scary. It could have taken me down at any time, but was getting closer all the time. I was sweating from nerves and scared for our baby. Noah held us both on the couch and we, or at least me, felt much the better for it.

Even the drop to the ground and the gunshot didn't seem to faze the little one. She was awake, but kept quiet. I checked her all over as soon as we were in the house to make sure I didn't smash her any when I went down. She was fine. What a day.

Chapter 16

We work on the hide the next day. I finish
skinning out the feet and we had cut the legs
to make them into a pair of boots. The head
I skin to make a nice over-the-head and
shoulders cape and cap in one out of. The
rest will be a pair of mitts from the front legs
and a blanket from the rest. It can always be
used for something else once it is tanned and
softened. The fur is super long and soft, so
it will be very nice as a blanket.

Roman and Thad walk over the next day
and see where we butchered the evening
before. The thought of us becoming late

lunch for a bear has them upset. I had a gun
with me, but had not wanted to stop and turn
around to see what was following me. I'm
just glad Noah was coming to meet me and
with a rifle.

We dragged the gut pile away from the area
well-traveled all winter and set snares out away
from it and some traps a bit closer in.

Elaine gets to ride along to feed chickens
and the goats, even milking the goats. She
giggles now at the feel of their fur against her
face. They whisker touch her face and she
giggles even more.

She has a little playpen Roman made for
her that I can move around the house easily.
In summer, it will be nice outdoors, even, as it
has a screen that covers it to protect from
bugs. Who knew when that pickup ignored
my signs at the driveway and pulled in that
"government guy" would become so
important a part of my life and we would end
up married and have a child together.
Certainly not me.

Thad gets a nice young bull moose before
rut and we all help butcher it out. He shares
it with everyone and is invited to dinner
everywhere he drops some off. He really
likes the chicken fried steak that Rose fixes
from moose and after she tells me how to
make it, it becomes my favorite also. It has
been a while since we had moose meat, and
everyone enjoys it. It just seems much harder

to find a nice young bull than it does to find bears or for the bears to find us.

We get the bear hams and bacon smoked before it gets too cold during the day. We have to bring it in at night so it doesn't freeze and not take a smoke. Then Noah and I bundle up Elaine and go delivering. Everyone gets a larger slab of bacon from this bear. The hams are huge, so we had sectioned them smaller before curing to make sure they took the cure to the bone. Some get boneless hams, some with bone in, but everyone gets a ham.

Roman shot a couple of large geese as they were flying south and planned on roasting them for Thanksgiving dinner. The weather was cold enough when he butchered them to be able to keep them that long. We would try to come over for dinner then.

Winter is wonderful. All the projects we worked on are completed, we have enough firewood and food stocked up to last until next harvest. We could relax and start new projects and work on some left over from last winter. We had a whole range of items to make for Elaine. A small sled we could pull, a small wagon she could ride in and a small chair she would be able to sit in on her own in a few more months.

She was rolling over and pulling herself into a sitting position. Her bottom became the indicator when the floor needed mopped.

Although once in a while I was inclined to dampen the diaper and let her do it. She scooted around on her bottom all the time. She was growing like a small weed. By Thanksgiving, she is sitting up pretty good on her own.

We bundle her up well and hike over to Kara's house. We have brought a few things I have been keeping back just for a special holiday. Olives, black ones and stuffed green ones. Kara is very happy to see them and makes sure everyone gets the same amount. She says she is almost happy enough to hug someone over the olives, she has missed them. She is not a huggy sort of person. Neither is her mom. They let you know how happy they are to see a person, but no just grabbing them for a hug unless you want a knee. It is pure reflex and they usually apologize, depending on who it is.

We enjoy a lovely dinner and the roast goose is very good. Far better than domestic goose, and they roasted it to a crispy perfection. The jelled lingonberry sauce went perfectly with it. Really good food was a treat although most of our food was very good and nutritious, it sometimes was repetitive. A nice special dinner now and then lifted everyone's spirits. The pies and the ice cream we brought along really topped the day and we all went home extremely over stuffed with good food.

As we walked home, the aurora came out in a spectacular display of colors and motion, wafting across the sky like giant chiffon curtains of changing colors, gently billowing in a solar breeze.   It was so beautiful, we stood and watched for several minutes until Elaine made a noise and we figured we should get her home and into bed.   She had enjoyed her day very much and behaved so well I couldn't believe it.   The twins, Dallas and Savannah were very interested in another small person.   They had never seen another baby before and were interested in everything. They were sturdy little ones and Shari was trying to potty train them, as she was tired of changing them.   No disposable diapers probably was going to make parents go back to training the children a lot younger than had been done in a couple of generations.   No more letting them wait until they were starting school from sheer laziness on the part of the parents to pay attention to the child and teach it something.

I think child raising was going to step back a few generations and to heck with Dr. Shmock. I know our child was going to grow up with consequences for her actions and to respect private property.   Just because something was cute when she was 2 didn't mean I would like it when she was 16.

We settled her in her bed after her evening singing from Daddy.   Then we sat at the front window and just watched the aurora display. No matter how many years I have lived here, it is always amazing and wonderful to watch. On a clear, still night, they make a dim crackling sound and the hairs raise up on the back of your neck and arms. Soon, we were enjoying each other more than we were watching the lights. It was a magical night.

As we finished a lingering kiss, I saw movement out in the edge of the trees. Not again. So I grabbed the rifle and opened the window just a little bit. The movement came again, more out in the open this time. Someone was sneaking towards the house. I raised the rifle and shot him. Noah fired from the other window and got the one coming in from that side. We left them lay until morning. If there were more hidden in the trees, we did not want to be targets as we came out the door. Usually we would have been asleep by now.

In the morning, Noah went out the back of the house through a window and circled around until he found the tracks where they came in. There were only the 2. When he got to them and flipped them over, they were frozen solid. But it was two of the roughest looking men I had ever seen in my life. There was no attempt at personal cleanliness. They were filthy and reeked of unwashed human. Even if they didn't have much, water was easy to come by up here. They could have kept a bit cleaner. At least if they had lice, they would have frozen out before we had to touch them. Under their rags on the outside, they were wearing body armor. Strange.

We loaded them onto the toboggan we used for hauling heavy loads over snow and took them out to the ditch we had used to cover the first two people the bear killed that were after us. Unfortunately, now the ground was frozen too hard to knock more of the bank down over these two. We did stack as many rocks as we could pry loose over them and snow.

I was tempted to set some traps and snares around them, but it felt a bit too ghoulish to do that. We had already pulled the traps from the bear gut pile. We would leave the snares and continue to check them regularly most of the winter.

I stayed in the house after we did the morning chores and Noah went to check on Roman and Thad. They also had midnight visitors. Theirs were also in the ditch along the main road. Thad was also watching the aurora from his window when he saw them sneaking in. The one that thought he would have an easy hostage in an old woman and tried grabbing Rose while she was out watching the aurora, made a bad mistake. Her grandson has taught her a few self-defense moves and she had him down and

gone so fast he never knew what hit him.   It
must have been a large group to hit every
house at the same time, even with only one or
two assailants.   Each of the cabins and
houses had been under attack.   For one
reason or another, it didn't succeed.   We were
up watching the aurora and making out.
There usually was always someone up at
Kevin's house, the same at Sam's and Paul's, at
night.   Kara was cleaning up after everyone
left fairly late.

Down at Will and Shari's, the twins were
too excited by the day to settle down, so they
were still up. Jeremy, Ashley, Dan and
Melanie were playing a game of cards and
Melanie got up for a drink and saw the
movement in the moonlight.   All were scruffy
looking, all wearing body armor under the
scruffy clothes.   This was planned and had a
chance of success.   Why would someone
target us and attempt to take on all of us at
one time?

Jeremy decided he would do some
scouting around and see where these people
all came from.   He backtracked them toward
town and found a very large area that had
been used as a camp and evidently for a few
days.

While circling the camp, he saw someone
coming back into the camp from the direction
of town.   He settled in and waited to see
what was going to happen next.   The new

arrival went to a shelter built into a small stand of trees and camouflaged with winter camo pattern. He had not expected that and might have missed it until he was right on top of it. He mentally shook his head thinking he better get back in practice. He carefully inched his wait to the back of the shelter and settled in again, to listen.

He could make out 2 voices. Not enough to hear exactly what was said, but enough to chill his blood. These people were planning on killing us all and setting up their own community using our supplies and homes. He was so intent on hearing all they were saying, he almost didn't hear the one coming up behind him. As the man reached down to grab him by the shoulder, he twisted around and yanked the man down and broke his neck before he could alert the others to his presence.

He tucked the man under the edge of some of the winter camo fabric laying in the brush and took his weapons with him as he inched away from the camp. The leaders apparently were not aware they were already missing 22 of their people. They appeared to be a camp of all men and that did not look good for their intentions to the women in our community.

Once Jeremy was far enough back and could again watch the camp, he used a small piece of the camo fabric he brought out from their camp.   Later in the day, 10 more men came into camp from the direction of town. That made 12 and 12 men could do a lot of damage to our community.

Jeremy came back to let us know what he had seen and we decided to attack before they could attack us again.   The next time we might not be so lucky.   Everyone decided Elaine and I should not go, neither should Shari and the twins.   What, leave us here not knowing and waiting to see what our fate was to be if they won?   Not on your life, Bud.

Even if we were lookouts up on the hill above the camp, we did not want to be left but did realize the small children may give us away.   One of the women at Sam's didn't want to go, so she volunteered to babysit.

No time like the present, so we gathered up arms and followed Jeremy back to the encampment.   We spread out and surrounded the camp, chose our targets and waiting until just after dusk.   Just to be sure we knew who we were dispatching, we chose a word to say as we touched someone and prepared to slash throats.   We thought we could tell them by the stench.   So far all we came near had a horrible aroma.

They were not any better up close while alive.   We slipped from bedroll to bedroll, cutting throats as we went.   Jeremy and Thad went into the big shelter.   Jeremy had some night goggles and the darkness in the shelter was not a problem for him. The apparent leader had a real bed set up in there and his aide was sharing it with him. Thad grabbed the aide as Jeremy handed him over by the scruff of the neck and had the leader cuffed and immobilized before he knew what was happening. A wide band of tape across his mouth made sure he didn't sound the alarm in case the job was not complete outdoors. There came a timid knock on a tree near the doorway of the shelter, and Thad turned on the light he brought with him. The inside of the shelter was a stockpile of military weapons and a few things Jeremy was surprised to see in civilian hands. Then he stopped and thought about it, with all the military bases in Alaska, why should it be a surprise?

He filled his backpack with the most dangerous items to remove them from the camp, tonight. Thad filled his also. Then as others checked in, he loaded their backpacks as well. None of this should be in the hands of their enemies.

Later, Jeremy wondered why he had not dispatched the leader the way the rest of the pack had been. A quick slash and done. Now they had 2 prisoners they had no place for and no use for.

Chapter 17

Back in Canada, Liz and her crew were having a fairly good winter. The weather wasn't being extremely cold and not an extreme amount of snow, either. The cattle were gaining weight and the horses looked very good. Even the chickens and turkeys were doing okay.

They had a nice Thanksgiving dinner to celebrate making it this far and in good condition. The new additions to their crew fit right in and were easy to get along with.

The elk herd continued coming into the fields and Liz continued to harvest one now and then to add to their diet. They were making a lot of jerky for travel food next Summer. The scrawny little orchard they passed just out of Whitehorse had given them several boxes of apples that they sliced and dried now. They played Johnny Appleseed and always planted the seeds when they could.

Just before Christmas, someone halloo'd the house and they went out to see who was coming. A couple of men walked up and introduced themselves. They were trying to start a community of other survivors a few miles south of here, along the old road going to Haines from Haines Junction. They would like to invite everyone to settle with them and of course bring the livestock with them. A deal was finally settled. Several of the cattle and a couple of the horses would stay. A few chickens and some turkeys so they could start their own herd and flocks.

They said they had plenty of feed and could trade feed for the animals. An older mare that was due to foal in the spring and another that didn't travel well was decided on to start their horse herd. A young stud would be left, also. Some cows were cut from the herd and one young bull. Liz made sure the Scottish highlander cattle they had picked up along the way stayed to go on north with them. The next day, they used one of the teams and a wagon to haul the crates with some chickens and turkeys and to bring back bags of feed. A few wanted to go, so they saddled up to drive the cattle and horses to their new home.

When they pulled over the hill and started down into the valley, it seemed a perfect spot to settle. Wide cleared fields and barns full of hay and grain, houses scattered across the valley and most showed signs of occupancy. It could be a very good community. The gates were open on a large pen near a very large barn showing signs of repairs. The people that met them at the barn were so happy to see them, they felt like celebrities.

The wagon was filled so heavily the horses had to work on pulling it home. When they returned to the barn, they pulled the horses right on in, with the wagon. After unhooking the horses and turning them out to roll, they checked some of the bags of feed on the wagon. Quite a bit of wheat, some corn, the rest about half and half, oats and barley. They loaded it evenly in the 4 wagons and covered it well. This would be great to grind for flour and meal.

Once in a while, people from the little community would come visit and it was nice to have neighbors again. All in all, it was a pleasant winter. Much time was spent mending harness and repairing the wagons and tractors. Clothes were made and others mended. Socks and underwear were fast becoming a premium item. Mary was knitting socks as fast as she could. The propane range helped make meals easier to prepare, it had a decent oven so a lot of baking was done.

One night, Tina tiptoed to her mothers' bed and whispered, "Goodnight Momma, I love you."

Sara hugged her tight and whispered back, "I love you too, goodnight."

It was the first time Tina spoke.

Chapter 18

Back in Alaska, we had a dilemma. Two
prisoners we didn't want. The aide confided
the men all smelled so bad because they did
not want to share the shelter with the leader.
He did not take kindly to being told no, and
everyone was afraid of him. He was rather
fastidious about some things and they did not
appeal when they were filthy and smelled.

The aide said one night when they were
without food, John had prepared a large roast
for them and after they ate it, he laughed and
told them that was the last person that told
him NO. No one was sure if he was telling

the truth or not, but no one went anywhere alone with him if they could help it.

The aide was just a kid, and was not with them of his own accord. John was afraid he would run off if he had a chance, so kept him in camp while the others robbed and killed.

Jeremy took John down to the river and chopped a hole in the ice, stuck his feet in and as it was getting very cold, waited a while for the ice to form around his legs. Once it was frozen securely, he left him to his fate. After hearing some of the stories of how he treated prisoners and even some of his own men, it was an easy way to go. Jeremy just couldn't bring himself to torture someone like that. He told John he would soon be meeting everyone he had ever wronged which seemed to scare John no end.

Jeremy didn't trust that something still couldn't go wrong, so stayed in the area a while and later went back to check. John Hiser was no more of a threat to anyone on this earth.

The small scavengers would take care of all the problems left laying around and most if not all would be gone before spring. Voles can leave just the hide and bones of an entire moose, they should be able to take care of a bunch of vermin.

Everyone felt a little ill after our night of vermin killing. It had to be done, but it wasn't something we could forget.

We were a subdued bunch for quite a while after that. The aide, Farren, was still here, but no one knew what to do with him. He seemed a nice kid, but could we trust him?

Al came over one day and asked if he could take Farren to his place. He needed some help and it was too hard for Natalie to do, now that she was expecting. No reason why not, if Farren didn't mind. He was just so glad to not be sent out on his own he agreed to go help. Al was doing very well on his trapline and he needed a skinner and someone to take care of the outside chores around the cabin.

Farren was good at following directions and helped out anywhere he could. That worked out well for both of them.

When he found out that Al was giving him a share in everything they took care of, besides room and board, he almost cried.

Everyone was content to have small private celebrations of Christmas at their own homes this year. No one felt comfortable leaving their homes unprotected now, after Thanksgiving. Just an hour one way or another, and we would have either walked in and found them in our homes, and been unprepared for an attack, or we would have been asleep and unprepared. Neither one appealed.

New Years dawned cold and getting colder. Then it settled deep into the valleys and crept up the hills until we were almost as cold as the valleys. Every time I have seen it do this, it usually lasts for quite a while. Every household had plenty of firewood to keep warm and there was no reason to have to spend much time outdoors. We dressed very warmly just to go do the barn chores and milk.

We kept the fire going 24/7 in the barn. There was always a large container of snow melting near the stove to have water for the goats. Water carried from the house would have been frozen solid before we reached the barn. A cup of boiling water tossed in the air vaporized before a drop hit the ground.

Our old fuel company thermometer wasn't digital but it did go to -80 on the scale. We never hit that cold at our house, but we were -40's, then one morning -56. Nose hairs freeze solid inside your nose at that and you always try to breathe through a facemask or scarf. Your eyelashes become crusted with frost from the moisture and warmth in your eyes, and if possible, it is safest to wear goggles to protect your eyes. Ears and noses are very vulnerable to frostbite, so need special care and coverage.

Any other time than the current one and worry about who it is coming through the door, most Alaskans used to leave the doors unlocked so anyone needing to come in, could. Standing still waiting for someone to unlock a door could mean death. So when someone staggered up onto the porch and gave a single thump on the door and thud on the floor, we hurried to let them in.

The person we ended up dragging in near the fire and prying out of their frozen clothes and parka turned out to be Melanie. We are shocked to see her out in this weather. We fill some pans with lukewarm water and start making sure her hands, feet and face are not frozen. They are close and it will be very painful while feeling returns, but no actual frostbite, just some frost nip. We have some heavy socks and a quilt near the stove, so when one of us comes in, we wrap in it to get warm. We now use it to wrap Melanie in. Soon she is sobbing and writhing in pain. A few small blisters form on her cheeks and a larger one on one toe.

Thawing out after partial freezing feels like being burned, and is extremely painful. We kept adding warm water as the water she was soaking in cooled. She continued to sob and finally was able to hold still but was still shivering, which is actually a good sign. When you are too cold to shiver, you are much too cold.

We asked if there was a problem and she said, "Yes, Dan is an insensitive beast and I can't stand to be around him another minute."

Hmmmm, maybe a touch of cabin fever setting in there. Once we know they have not been attacked and no one is ill or injured, we act as if it is no big deal and an ever day occurrence for us to have frozen women dropping in.

We keep her bundled up in warm blankets and add a bear fur under her on the couch. The barn kittens have learned to be nice little housecats, and are nestled all around her, adding their warmth and purring. Once she is warmed and comfy, she falls asleep.

We go take care of the chickens so she won't overhear us, and wonder how we can let Dan know she is alive and well. He has lived here long enough to know how dangerous it is to go out in these temperatures. She must have been really fed up to walk out in this weather. But cabin fever is seldom rational. Partners have been known to cut everything they own right down the middle, including the stoves, chairs, beds and bedding. Some have marked lines down the middle of the home and on everything in it.

Where Melanie doesn't do any outdoor work in the winter and seldom ventures out at all, she is a prime candidate for it. Being outside, even in the few hours of sunlight in the middle of winter seems to help stave off the symptoms. Keeping busy and getting exercise seems to help, also.

When Noah goes out to milk and do the other barn chores, he starts a good fire in the stove in the little cabin. If Melanie wants to be alone, we can give her alone. Once she has eaten, we bundle her back up and he escorts her out to the cabin, tells her where the woodshed is, and leaves her there. The cabin is nice and warm and she should be comfortable. There is dry food stored in there and Noah set a chunk of ice in a pot on the stove to thaw for water. Another in a pot on the counter to thaw for drinking and a bucket of snow melting to use for washing up.

When either of us go to the barn to milk or feed, we wave and keep going. The same when we get firewood. She is fine with this for about a week.

When Noah goes out to milk one morning, he hears a pssst, from in the loft. He climbs up and finds Dan camped by the chimney of the woodstove in fine comfort. Dan is used to traveling in extreme cold and made the hike over in fine form. Probably not something to let Melanie know yet. She is still peeved. We figure when she is in a better mood, she will come back over to the house and talk. Dan has been over several times already to make sure Melanie is okay. This is just the first time he has let anyone know he is here.

Dan says he will leave some food on her porch during the night but is going home to take care of the place and the dogs. He will check back every other day or so to make sure she is okay but will only come in the barn so she don't see him.   He doesn't want to upset her any more than she was.

A couple of days later, when I go out to milk, Dan is back in the barn.   He asks if Melanie has said anything about why she is so upset or is she even coming out of her exile. We know she is coming out to get wood and dump the slop and honey buckets and get more snow to melt for washing up.   Food placed in the box on the porch is gone when Dan brings more for us to place there.   We figure she will want to talk to someone one of these days.

After about 2 weeks, she must have finally gotten tired of her own company.   The weather has warmed up a bit and she comes over and knocks on the door.   I let her in and Noah suddenly has something needing done out in the barn.

"Wow, that was subtle, wasn't it?"   I ask.

She isn't smiling, but she isn't crying or frowning either, so that is a plus.   She sits down over near the heater and fidgets around a bit.   Finally she blurts out that Dan doesn't really love her.   As besotted as he always seems to be, I wonder how she has decided that.

Then she goes on about how it was always her pursuing him, and he just got in the habit of her being around and they drifted into getting married since it seemed the thing to do.   I asked her if she was the one that proposed marriage and she is shocked I would think her capable of that. All I could say was she was the one that said she did all the pursuing. I figured he had enough of a mind of his own, that he certainly would not have proposed unless he actually wanted to be married to her.

She thought that over a while and admitted when she went to visit him, she usually always dragged one of the other girls along. He was around them as much as he was around her and he was the one that proposed. So maybe he did actually love her. He never had came right out and said the words though. I asked her if she ever had, either. "Well, no, but the guy is supposed to say it first."

"Does he help you around the place and do things to make life nicer for you?"

"Yes, he does, but he is a nice guy, he does nice things for everyone."

Somehow I don't think he would do the same things for just anyone.

Soon she starts to worry whether he is okay and why hasn't he checked to see if she is okay if he loves her. I'm not sure he wants her to know he has been over almost every other day since she got here.

By the time Noah comes in, Melanie is almost ready to walk home. Now indecision has her waffling back and forth go, stay, go, stay. Noah goes right back out to the barn. When he comes back, Dan is right behind him.   Melanie doesn't see him as she has her back to the door when Noah and Dan walk in.   She is telling me she loves Dan, but she can't stay with him if he doesn't love her also.

Dan walks up behind her and wraps his arms around her to hug her and gets a stomp on the instep and an elbow in the belly.   As he doubles over in pain, he groans, "Just one of the reasons I love you so much, woman, you really know how to give a guy a good time."

"You love me?   Now, you tell me you love me?   I wait here in agony 2 long weeks wondering if you are okay, if you are eating right, if you are missing me at all and you waltz in here and just finally tell me you love me?"

"Sweetheart, I brought you food every other day to check on you and make sure you are okay.   I was so scared when I couldn't find you the first night.   I searched all over our place and went to Will and Shari's, then Jeremy and Ashley's.   Then Kara's place and checked with Rose.   Roman and Thad's and each of the other places there, also.   By the time I got here, everyone was asleep, so I slept in the barn and saw you at the cabin the next day.   I had to go home and keep our place from freezing up and take care of the animals. But I have been back often."

Melanie sits down on the couch and is thinking this all over.   This has been a tough time on her and she isn't sure what to think. Noah and I go in our room to check on Elaine in her crib and leave them alone. Maybe we will be losing our guest today, or maybe not. Soon we hear raised voices and a door slam. Oh well.

When we come back out of the bedroom, Dan is gone and Melanie is stomping her way back to the cabin.

Slowly the weather warms up a bit and we bundle up the baby and head out to check snares and the few traps we still have out. Not much was moving during the extreme cold so most of the traps are empty and we pull them. We find one wolf in a snare and take it home to thaw and skin.

When we got home, we propped the wolf in the corner on a tarp to thaw and unbundled Elaine. She was growing so fast I couldn't believe it. She was pulling herself up to stand and take a few steps as long as she was hanging on to something. She was already learning when we said no, to not touch. It was far better for her to learn easily now, than to have hard lessons later when it could mean life or death. Besides, I did not want to raise a spoiled rotten, entitlement- oriented child.

Chapter 19

Dan started leaving little presents on Melanie's porch but didn't try to see her again. He couldn't find actual flowers this time of year, so made some fur flowers from scraps of fur that were really cute. I think he was making progress on getting her to see that yes, he really did love her.

One day, she came over to the house while Noah was in the barn, carrying her bouquet of fur flowers. She asked me how I knew for sure that I was pregnant. I told her until it started kicking me, I wasn't sure and just ignored the other symptoms. After a while, it is impossible to ignore. She held up the flowers and asked if I had ever seen anything cuter. Each flower had a tiny face in the middle and a little tag saying I Love You. The man must have spent hours making those.

When Noah came in a bit later, Dan was behind him and the men were talking and didn't notice Melanie sitting with me on the couch. Dan sounded so sad, even I noticed and I am not the most sensitive of persons. When Dan saw Melanie sitting there, his face lit up and there was a movie moment when anyone looking just knew they belonged together.

She stood up and walked over to him, wrapped her arms around him and leaned her head against his shoulder. He wasn't too sure whether it was safe to hug back or not but took the chance and hugged her to him.

They just stood there a while, then he asked if she would please come home with him. He missed her too much to keep staying there alone and didn't think we wanted permanent tenants in our little cabin.

She nodded agreement and they went over to pack her few belongings and came back to say thanks and headed home.

Well, that certainly was not the way I expected to spend January. Certainly was something to keep us from also getting a bit of cabin fever ourselves, but since we spend a bit of every day outdoors, I don't worry too much about it. We have too much to do to get bored.

The cheese making is something I am enjoying very much. I wish I had some cultures to make some of the hard cheeses. I'm just glad I can make the soft ones. Mozzarella is the hardest I can make without a culture to start it with. I might try a few variations to see if I can manage a harder cheese when I know I can do this consistently without feeding the chickens too many batches. At least we can still have pizza.

I am a little sad that I won't have any baby pictures of Elaine to look at when she is grown up. Just one more thing we will never do again. Sometimes I feel like starting a list of never agains. But that would be depressing and it is very important right now for us to all stay as upbeat and positive as possible. A bad attitude could infect the whole place.

Now that Melanie is back home, we fall back into our routine. We brush the goats and the caribou as much as we have time for and save the hair in bags. We do the same with the dogs and cats. Maybe we can make yarn from it to knit items we will be needing.

If nothing else, we can make felt using it. It worked with horse hair placed in a large bag and smoothed out to use as a saddle pad. Sweat and the pressure of the saddle eventually made it into a nice felt pad made of the horse's own hair. After taking it out of the bag, the edges were trimmed to shape and it was very nice. No reason boot liners can't be made the same way.   If we manage to make enough, maybe we could make the felt winter boots and mitts used in Scandinavian countries.   I remember that it took a lot of hair to make a pad thick enough to use as a saddle pad on a horse.   Another thing to experiment on.

Every day that is not extremely cold, we bundle up and go outside.   We cut poles and stack to build more fence or use as rafters, depending on what our next projects end up being.   No matter what, we can always use more poles.

We are training the goats to be tethered out.   They don't care much for it, but it gives them browsing on brush time and helps clear along the driveway and yard.   Then we can cut more hay in the summer to feed the goats. I see a vicious cycle here.

All the animals, goats, caribou and dogs anyway, the cats won't participate, have learned to carry at least a small pack and drag small weights.   Noah is building a very small cart for Elaine and training a goat to pull it. The older nanny seems to be the best natured for that job.

When I used heads of cabbage this winter, I saved the hearts and didn't cut into them.   I trimmed the bottoms, allowed them to dry a bit, stuck some toothpicks in them to hold them in a glass of water and sprouted them. Then I set them in trays of soil.   I am hoping to get them to produce seed heads so we can continue to grow cabbage. If nothing else, we will have very small cabbage heads where each leaf was attached. I am doing this with carrots, also, only using the bottom of each, keeping the top end and sprouting it.

We all try to be more alert to possible dangers from other people coming around. It is very hard to pay attention to what a person is doing and also to whether or not anyone is sneaking up on you. I felt sorry for Al and Dan. They were the first places anyone would hit, from the north or the south.

We stretched string around in the brush with empty tin cans and a few pieces of gravel in them to possibly let us know if anyone was in our woods. Usually we found moose, bear, even squirrels messing with the string or cans. The dogs were our best early warning system. Along the main roadway, we wove the willow and young birch trees into a mesh of trees. We used strips of bark to tie them in place. After a while, they will grow into each other. We don't want to set booby traps that will injure animals or ourselves. In summer, the electric barb wire fence will go back up.

After seeing how well the thermal mass rocket type heater is working for Paul, I think everyone out here is interested in building one for themselves. It would certainly stretch our wood supply out better. If we can find some clay around here, we will probably build one into our house. So many plans, so much to do. I guess we have time, since we aren't going anywhere.

Al stopped over to see how we were doing. He was enjoying married life and even enjoyed having the boy staying with them. He wasn't sure he was ready to be a Dad yet, but since babies never wait until parents are ready, he would soon know for sure. Anyone that would rescue a baby caribou and carry it miles to safety, would certainly care for his own child, I figured.

I packaged up some things to use with the baby for him to take home when he left. Plus filling his pack with cheese and ice cream would make a load for him going home.

This must be our month for having visitors as the next day, Roman and Thad hiked over. They were surprised at how much Elaine had grown in the short time since they seen her last. She was a bit shy at first, but soon was perched on Grandpa's lap and enjoying it. She takes it as her due that everyone adores her. We don't disappoint.

I fixed a lunch for us and while we were eating, the dogs started barking. Noah checked out the window and saw Will, Shari and the twins coming in the drive. We set more places at the table and as they came in, told them they were late. The twins were walking very well and running all over the place.   Shari said they even walked part of the way over, instead of staying on the sled.   The deep snow caught them a few times if they got off the packed trail.   Shari had more clothes for Elaine in the pack she carried. She was excellent at sewing and made such nice clothes for her children that I felt honored to have them for mine.   At the bottom of the bundle, was a very nice shirt she had made for me.   I was surprised and pleased to have such a lovely shirt.   I certainly wouldn't want to wear it while working, so it just became my new best shirt for special occasions.

She was using up her skirts and dresses to make over into new clothes and made something for each person out here. She wanted to thank us for helping her so much.   From a delicate Southern Belle, she was now a tough Alaskan Woman.   Her words, not mine.   She is really a nice woman and I enjoy her company.

For dessert, we pull out some of the ice cream we have been experimenting on.   That really hits the spot, even though it is the middle of winter and a lot of snow anywhere we look outdoors.

Our little gathering has a festive air and we all enjoy the afternoon very much.   When everyone is getting ready to leave, we pack up more cheese and ice cream to send home with them.

Since it takes 5 gallons of goat milk to make 1 pound of butter, we don't make it very often and haven't had enough to share. But I need some of the buttermilk as part of making cheese, not the mozzarella, so we do make butter once in a while. If I can figure out a way to use all the buttermilk in making cheese, we will make more butter.

Chapter 20

In Canada, Liz and her group were helping the Canadians get their community working and improving their chances of survival. The gunsmith was helping them learn how to make firearms to protect themselves and to hunt the numerous elk and deer for meat. Then the cattle they traded for would be used to increase their herds and possibly some could be trained to milk, although they were not milk cows.

The veterinarian in the little community was training Marsha to be a vet. She was very good with animals and had a knack for it.

Richard and Mike were helping build a wood gasifier to run an old tractor one of the people had on their property. Once they found out how many supplies there were on hand for building something like that, they also converted an old gas engine to run a sawmill.

The winter was spent in learning and working. Mary was still knitting socks by the dozen and several of the women were learning how from her. She also taught them how to spin yarn. Liz taught classes in nutrition and preparing and canning their harvests and crops.

One of the fellows in the community was very interested in Sara. She was very leery of him or any other man that looked at her. He spent the winter stopping by to talk to her and helped as much as he could, in whatever chores she was working on. He slowly was winning her over, with his gentle manner and thoughtfulness. The day that Tina was happy to see him show up and said Hi to him, went a long ways toward Sara allowing him to stay around more.

As winter started easing up and some of the snow melted, preparations began for the trail north. Sara told her guy she was moving to Alaska and he said fine, he would like to go, also. They asked Liz and Richard and they were okay with that. A couple of the other young men wanted to come along, also, and as they were polite and helpful, they were not turned away.

Another wagon was built out of parts

located in the area and hooked behind one of the tractors. It would be a light load, crates for the chickens and turkeys they still had after sharing some with the community and eating a few over the winter. More elk and deer were harvested and made into jerky. Some of the hams were cured and smoked to be used along the way, also. Several were harvested for the community also and they were shown how to cure and prepare the meat to keep.

By the time the grass was growing enough to supply feed along the trail, the wagons were all loaded and the whole community turned out to see them off.

The road north was not too bad except for potholes that were there before the quake. The 3 winters since had not improved them at all. The tractors and teams had to be careful not to break an axle falling into some of them. In some areas it was better to drive along beside the road instead of in the road.

By the time they reached the long bridge across the Tanana River, the ice was long gone and the river was back down to a very low level. The bridge did not appear to be damaged but it was easier to cross the river than to attempt it. As they were crossing, they could see the underside of the bridge and found they were doing the right thing. Several of the support beams were cracked and dangling.

After that, they crossed most of the longer spans by going down and crossing in the rivers. It was more difficult for the tractors and wagons, but safer in the long run. One of the bridges appeared to have been sabotaged and after crossing the river, they found some people waiting in ambush. The ambush was ruined by the herd simply walking right over them. To add insult to injury, one of the dogs bit one of the fellows when he swung a stick at the dog. Then Shirley kicked the man in the back of the head from her horse for hitting her dog.

They pushed the herd a bit farther up the road that day, to put some miles between them and the ambushers. They may not have been well organized, but they could still cause problems and be sneaky about it.

The summer trip went very well with only a few minor problems. They were able to stop and rest the herd whenever they found enough feed to keep them in good shape.

Autumn was approaching as they neared the Delta Junction area. They decided to check around for folks in the area and any grain or hay barns still standing. They did find some large fields of volunteer grain that they let the cattle and horses eat on. They hooked their tractors to some of the farm equipment they found and harvested as much as they could and stacked the bales, then tarped them with the heavy duty tarps they found in the ruins of a large barn. The main house was in fair condition, so they decided to spend the winter right there. A crew was sent around the fence lines to check and repair any downed fence. The fence crew spotted a herd of bison and reported back at the house. Soon there was a bison to butcher out for some excellent eating. The nights were getting cold enough to keep the meat a while so they used as much as possible fresh. Roasts and steaks were a welcome change from jerky and cured meat. Even the burger was greeted with pleasure.

The hide was very large, so they pegged it out and spent hours scraping and fleshing on it. Then they spread the brains on it, hoping to tan it that way. Every day, they worked on the hide and kept scraping it thinner in the middle to make it more flexible.

While riding around the area, looking for more barns and equipment, they found a family living in a small house. Once over the initial shock for the family of seeing friendly people on horseback, they came out to talk. There was someone at the window and they were probably covered by a rifle for the talk, but in these times, that was only common sense.

Marsha rode back to the house and put a couple of the hens and a rooster in a crate and took it back with her. Liz rode back with her and as they came up near the house, the woman of the house saw the chickens and grabbed her husband by the shoulder. She told him no thieves were going to bring them live chickens.

The thought of eggs and future chickens brought smiles to the faces of the family living there. Then when they offered them some cows and a horse, they had new best friends. They said they had just become the wealthiest folk in the neighborhood. There are several folks living in a loose group here, and the group from Oregon are just beyond the area they have been using. It was considered a no man's land between this group and the group that tried to ambush the herd.

It was quite a while back since they had marauded around here at all, so they may have finally ran out of bullets. Since no shots were fired toward the herd or people, it was agreed possibly, they had.

It looked like this winter would be similar to last winter. Helping the folks here convert a couple of tractors over to wood gasification, holding a few classes and teaching nutrition and preserving foods.

Shortly after meeting this group of people, another group showed up at the edge of the fields, waving a white flag. They were allowed to proceed into the yard and a couple of Liz's group went out to talk to them. They were from the ambushers. They were tired of living like animals and starving most of the time, they wanted to settle and start living like people again. They wanted to know if they could move to the farm area just south of this one and start learning how to make it as farmers. No one could promise they could actually do that, but they could be taught the basics and given a start. They were sent off with some bison meat to share at their camp and the possibility of some help, if they were in earnest.

The next morning, there was an entire encampment parked under the edge of the trees where the flag wavers had been, yesterday.

It was decided to help them get settled on the other farm. Some of them were picked to come over every day to learn how to care for the animals and birds. They had some food and were rationing it out. Winter not even begun and they were short on food.

One of the women said the salmon should still be running down at the river and she knew where some nets used to be stored near there. So a crew of them started out to see if they could net enough salmon to dry and use for the winter. There were enough caught before freeze-up to add variety to the diets and supplement other sources of protein.

More were told to start gleaning the volunteer grains in the old farm fields to use as porridge and grind for flour.

Some bags of grain were found in an old storage facility. Rodents had been chewing on the bottoms of a few of the bags, but the rest were in good condition. The chewed bags were turned over and retied. It would still work for poultry feed. The undamaged bags would feed people quite well. The teams and wagons made the rounds and gathered as much hay and grain as they could find. Several bags were delivered to the new neighbors.

The new neighbors and the established group were very unsure of each other. Liz figured they could get over it if they wanted classes and assistance from them. They would teach, they would not support freeloaders.

Most of the new group were willing to get right in and help in any way possible. What they didn't know, they asked about and learned.

Both groups were in the same classes as Liz refused to hold separate classes for them. They were going to be neighbors for the rest of their lives in all likelihood and it was dumb to keep up old feuds.

Slowly, new friendships developed and the two groups started working together. By Christmas time, everyone was getting along quite well and since Liz's group was centrally located, they decided to have a Christmas program there. Richard would write and deliver a sermon since he is very good at it. The younger folks and children would put on a program to entertain the adults.

There were several children in both groups, so there would be lots of shepherds and angels. Every child that wanted a part would have one. The event would be as magical with the story of His birth as it could be made. The main barn was repaired and the largest area available, so wood heaters would be set up in it and the barn would become the auditorium for that night.

The children practiced with enthusiasm and a few even had some talent in singing the lovely old Christmas carols. Someone had a guitar and someone else had a violin, so they played along with the singers.

Another bison was harvested shortly before Christmas, so several roasts were prepared. Enough eggs had been saved up to make a very large batch of noodles. A rich broth was made from the pan juices of the roast and small amounts of dried vegetables and herbs added to make it filling and delicious. After the noodles were added, it made a lovely side dish for the roasts. Oat cakes were made from the oats gleaned from the fields. They were sweetened and dried berries added to have as a dessert. It was not a traditional Christmas dinner, but it was enjoyed and shared by all. It was served at noon, the program followed and then everyone went home in the fast approaching darkness.

The winter proceeded as they usually do, whether one is ready for them or not. Everyone was too busy to have time for sulking or focusing on what they didn't have. The arrival of the cattle, horses, chickens and some turkeys gave everyone hope that they were going to not only survive, but survive and thrive. Learning how to raise the animals and birds helped raise their spirits even more.

Services were held every Sabbath and many came that never stepped foot in any gathering before, not only came, but learned.

Two of the men studied with Richard to learn more so they could continue the services after he moved on.

A study curriculum was set up to help teach the children so reading and writing would not be forgotten. Who knew what shape the land masses had settled into? The old maps of the world would not have much meaning to anyone from now on.

Liz figured they only had about 3 weeks more travel to reach Rose and her family, if they still lived. They would travel slowly when spring arrived, but had to make it early enough to supply feed for the animals for the next winter. They had utilized many of them and traded or given away quite a few, also. But there was still a lot of animals to handle and feed. So they planned throughout the winter.

Chapter 21

Back in Alaska, winter moved along
relentlessly. The days were getting longer, so
we could work outdoors in daylight instead of
dusk.

We started early on falling trees towards
next winter's wood. It was easier to skid the
lengths home on snow than to drag through
the dirt, later. The sap wasn't coming up yet,
so the wood was fairly light, comparatively
speaking. The dogs were getting their
workout dragging wood, Elaine was enjoying
riding on the sled we used to pull her around
everywhere.

We still had gas that worked for the
chainsaws, so firewood was not as hard as it
would get in the future when the gas ran out.
Since we didn't use it frivolously, I hoped that
would be quite a while away, yet. I wasn't

sure how long the stabilizer would work in the barrels I had stored in the woodshed. Noah was amazed at how much we had stored in there. Well, I like to be prepared. Looks like it was a good thing. I just don't know what others do that didn't stock up when they had any spare money. I pretty much always had to buy as much ahead as possible, since I didn't have a real job and no steady income. I was very lucky to own my property and it not being in an organized Borough, no property taxes. Just one very good job up north made that possible. Not going to have those again any time in the next 100 years at least.

Noah and I were talking about it one day and thought if we ever had a means, whether it would be something to investigate going north and checking on what could be done to start up the crack plant at Prudhoe and make gas again. Just a thought.

One day while talking to Al, it is brought up again. He says we don't have to go that far for gas, there is a tanker full sitting at the Yukon Bridge and the underground tanks should still be full, also.

Since this winter isn't one of the really deep snow winters, the guys talk it over with Roman and Thad and Dan. Dan is all for starting up his plane and flying them up to check it out. So we use enough of my stored gas to make the round trip, just in case. They take a small generator and a battery charger up with them.

Later, Dan tells us no one has touched anything around the bridge area. The camp is still intact except some collapsed areas. The shop is still standing and the tanker truck is right where Al said it would be. There were 2 more tankers on the other side, one had diesel and the other was a propane delivery truck. They got them all started and brought them across the ice on the river rather than trust the long bridge. They pumped fuel up from the underground tank for the plane and topped off both the tanks on it. At the old Pump station on the south side of the bridge, they discovered a plow truck, so they fueled it up and were plowing the road ahead of the trucks and walking back to bring up the trucks.

Since they only had to plow one lane of the road and the snow filled in the potholes, it was actually pretty good road. They checked each bridge as they came to it, and only one appeared too dangerous to attempt. Using the plow as a road builder around the bridge worked fairly well. They were able to cross the stream on ice and come on down. They should arrive soon.

While checking the shop at the bridge, they loaded up on all the oil and additives. They hung the trucks with tires and tools. The seats were full of clothing from the shop in the camp. The sleepers on the trucks were filled with blankets, sheets, pillowcases and pillows. The clothes were mostly T shirts and sweatshirts and pants, but they were new. The back of the shop in the camp was collapsed and animals were getting in, so the clothes and bedding would soon have been ruined if left. Some of the large kitchen utensils and containers were brought back and would be shared around. They thought the cloth items should be brought first to keep them from being destroyed, the metal, glass and plastic stuff could be brought at some later date if needed.

When the propane truck arrived, I think I appreciated it the most. Al took the truck around from place to place, filling all the bottles and pickle barrel tanks everyone in our community had.

Thad was driving the tanker of gasoline. He parked it and everyone brought containers to him. My old pickup started right up and we loaded the empty barrels we had on hand. After unloading ours, we hauled for everyone else, also.

Jeremy was driving the tanker of diesel, and we didn't have an immediate need for it, although it would come in handy later. Both of the tanker trucks and the propane truck were parked along the main road between properties on a fairly level stretch of road. It wasn't like they would block any traffic. The plow truck was parked at Al's. He said he always wanted one of those.

Noah and I bundled up Elaine and took the old pickup and a trailer and went back up the road before the ice melted and the road closed with snow. We had the come-alongs and straps and wanted to see if we could load the propane pickle barrel tanks left at the shop and the camp. The pickup had the snowplow I used in the old days on the front, so we were able to make the bypass roads a bit better around the bridges. We stopped first at the Pump Station and looked around. There was a front end loader, besides the plow they had taken to plow the road.

Noah worked on it a while and got it running. It had a full tank of fuel, so we took it across the river to load the tanks on our trailer. The smaller tank was loaded first, and then we found the stack of building supplies behind the shop, so instead of loading the other tank on the trailer, he loaded the building supplies. The other tank, he picked up in the bucket of the loader and we were ready to start home. He had to use the loader to pull my pickup up the steep bank on the other side of the river with the loaded trailer.

We drove slowly home. The bed of the pickup was full of the blankets that would need washed and the other supplies the guys left that needed cleaning. In the years ahead,

they may be needed very much.   A little bit
of rodent urine could be washed off this
summer.   Drying on the line in the sun would
help, also.   The sweatshirts with chewed holes
in them could be cut down and made into
children's clothes very easily.   So could the T
shirts and sweatpants.   I would start hand
washing the clothing tomorrow.   I already
had plans for Elaine's new sleepers.

I picked out several of the cutest shirts and
washed them the next morning.   As soon as
they were dry, over the heater, I started
cutting out the sleepers I wanted to make.   I
made some for Natalie and Melanie, and some
for Dallas and Savannah, also, besides the
ones I wanted to make for Elaine.   From the
parts I cut off, I make little hoods for them,
too.   Something over their heads at night will
help them stay warmer.   By the time Noah
comes in that evening, I have a couple of
them completed.   Some of the scrap made a
doll for Elaine and she is playing with it.   So I
make dolls for the others.   They look more
like sock monkeys only made from the arms
of sweatshirts.   So I add ears and muzzles
and we have sweatshirt puppies.   With the
material wrong side out, it is soft and a little
fuzzy.   The tails aren't too great, but they are
tails.   There aren't many toys around for the
children, so we make do.

The blankets that had chew marks and torn
areas, were washed and cut down to make

blankets for babies. I hemmed them up on my old sewing machine. Some of the thin quilts used at the camp as bedspreads, I cut into diaper sized pieces and hemmed. They should be absorbent, anyway.

I use assorted colors to make small sleepers for the ones not born yet, and a small puppy for them, also. Then we start delivering the things we gathered and made. Natalie is due any minute and very happy to have some more things for her baby. I showed her what I intended on the diaper pieces and she thought maybe she would make a few more from some of their old blankets.

Shari was in the middle of playing in a tent camp they were building with sheets and blankets in her living room. She was a bit embarrassed to be caught under the table with a child in each arm. But all embarrassment fled when she looked at what we brought for her twins. She liked the idea of attached hoods as it was hard to be sure they were warm enough all night. The toys fascinated them both and soon they were playing with their new "puppies". Elaine watched wide eyed as Dallas and Savannah ran around the room and ducked under sheets. Soon she was pulling herself up and hanging onto the couch, she took a few steps after them. They thought she was a new toy and proceeded to hang onto her hands as she walked a few steps out into the room.   She plopped onto her bottom and crawled on after them under the sheets and they all played happily for a while.

She was not happy to leave her new friends and they were not happy to see her go.   We still needed to stop and see Melanie and give her the things we brought for her.

Melanie greeted us at the door and looked very good.   She oohed and aahed over the little sleepers and blankets and said she would probably need to make herself a lot more but did still have a few months.   She was showing a bit now, but was happy about it.

Dan was making a cradle for her and she couldn't get over how much they both looked forward to the little one.   I showed her how to use the sleeper as a pattern to make more like it.   She thought she had some T shirts that should be retired to sleeper status.   Now that there were some new ones to replace them with, she didn't feel so bad about cutting them up.

Chapter 22

By the time we left Melanie, it was still light but the sun was down. Elaine was completely worn out from all the outdoor travel and playing today. As we neared home, something seemed wrong. We hurried around the curve and saw smoke. Noah ran for the house and got the door unlocked. He grabbed the tub of melting snow we keep near the heater and threw it on the pile of scraps near the stove that somehow got tipped onto the side of the stove and were smoldering away.

The house was full of smoke and we could hear the cats meowing from somewhere in the bedrooms after they heard our voices. We opened all the windows and doors. The inside of the house was coated in smoke and everything in it smelled. This was going to take some major house cleaning. We would have to stay in the cabin tonight.

While Noah pulled the mass of burnt material outside, I went on over and started a fire in the heater in the cabin. It would heat up fairly fast, but the mattresses would be cold clear through, so I removed all blankets and placed them over the chairs to warm them and the mattresses.

The chickens were okay but not happy. They got some smoke through the vents, but not enough to hurt them a lot.

We are going to have to quit leaving home. It seems like every time we do, something happens that isn't all that great. Nothing happened when we went after the stuff at the Yukon, but Thanksgiving wasn't so great, now this.

All I can figure out is maybe the pets were playing around and dragged the material too close to the stove.

Elaine is too tired to complain much about not having her own bed to sleep in. By the time we fall into bed, so are we. We will have to scrub and clean everything in the house. The cats are not happy in the small cabin with us, but they also were not happy in the house with the smoke. They are all smoky and I wipe them off with a damp cloth to help clean their fur, which they also don't like. The dogs don't mind the getting wiped down.

The smoke in the air has all cleared out by the next day and we start cleaning.

Everything not nailed to the walls is hauled outdoors. Clothes and blankets are draped over the clotheslines after beating them on the snow. Throw rugs are beaten in the snow and placed over the fence. Anything fur is rubbed in snow and shaken, then rubbed in snow some more. All our winter gear is beaten in the snow.

Once we are down to bare walls and floors, we start on the ceiling and clean as much as we can on it. Then down the walls. The kitchen is wiped down as much as possible, then all the floors get mopped. The stove is kept stoked to dry as we go. Elaine's crib was the first thing we cleaned and dried, so she is stuck in it all day. She is not very happy about it, but she thinks adults are odd anyway, so she settles down and plays with her toy. She has a chunk of jerky to chew on for her teeth.

The bedding kept our mattress from too much smoke, none on it, but it did smell. So it was still outdoors, airing out. We beat snow into it whenever we had a few extra minutes from indoors. By evening, it was smelling pretty fresh so we took it back indoors.

We fixed some dinner and decided we would sleep in our house tonight, not the cabin. We brought the cats back over and they suspiciously sniffed every room and checked out all the bare space. Our couch was still outside, so were the chairs and table. The books were in the barn with my paintings. I didn't know whether we could salvage all of them or if they would be kept in the cabin from now on. The ones in my covered shelves only had odor so they would eventually make it back in.

The chickens still weren't very happy, but when the sun was still out, I checked in their coop and it didn't look bad at all. I brought in some extra grain and gravel and they seemed to cheer up. I wasn't as easily cheered.

I know it could have been much worse. We could have lost it all. Even the pets are okay. Now it was just a lot of hard work to salvage all we could. We had tubs of snow melting near the stove, so Elaine still had to stay in her crib. We couldn't take a chance of her falling in a tub.

Noah and I were moving our couch back in the house after 2 days of beating snow into it and leaving it outdoors to air, when Roman and Thad showed up.

They wanted to know why we didn't come get them to help us clean up. We just looked at each other and started to laugh. We truly had not thought of going for help.

Roman started cleaning up the old sewing machine. He said the smoke could make it rust inside and not work the next time I used it. Since I oiled it regularly, it wasn't bad inside   The guns were always wrapped in blankets, so they were in pretty good shape anyway, but he disassembled them and cleaned, anyway.

Thad helped Noah move the rest of the furniture back into the house.   I am checking on the clothes that had been in drawers and only needed aired out.   Quite a bit is fine to bring back in.   The hairs on my neck feel like they are standing on end and I slowly look over to the edge of the trees.   A huge grizzly is just standing there looking at me.   He isn't acting threatening, more of a curiosity thing. I already have my arms full of clothing, so I back slowly toward the house, but talking steadily to the bear.   He loses interest in my conversation and heads deeper into the woods.   I must have looked almost as scared as I am, when I reached the house.   When I tell the guys about the bear, they go over and look but see no sign other than his tracks. We would have to keep an eye out for him and our barn animals and the caribou.   Later, when we check his tracks, he just kept on a straight course for the top of the hill.   We just happened to be on his path.   We never see him again, either.

Noah, Roman and Thad all got in and help wash the bedding and outdoor gear we have to wash.   We string more clothesline using small rope.   Some will just have to be left on the lines until it thawed and dried or freeze dried. They could certainly wring it out better than I do. Two guys on a quilt can almost wring it dry.

By the time they go home, we are in much better condition than we expected to be. With the weather warming up, we will soon need to start tapping the birch trees for sap and boiling it down for syrup. So while we are doing all this cleaning, we gathered all our buckets, tubing and taps, and scalded and dried them, also.

We have more than enough firewood on hand to boil off the sap, no matter how much we gather this year. We are going to start as soon as possible, and go just as long as we can. So much depends on weather for gathering sap to boil. Too cold and it doesn't run, too warm and it turns bitter. I want to have enough on hand to last all year and maybe trade or use as gifts. Everyone enjoyed the candy made last year, so even that was a possibility if we get enough.

A couple of days later, we decide to tap a couple of trees and see if they are ready. As soon as the tap is in, the sap almost squirts out, so we hook up the tubing and get a bucket hung to gather sap. We set out all our taps and by the time we are done, the first buckets are ready to dump. As the temperatures drop toward evening, the sap slows and we head home. Elaine really enjoyed the day of tromping through the snow in the woods in her carrier. Mom on the other hand is beat.

We check the fire under the boiling sap pans and add more wood. We have the electric fence up and working since seeing the bear. We hope it would deter him or any other bear from checking out the syrup or the animals.

The next 10 days are hectic but productive. We manage to make several jars of syrup and some candy, also. More than enough for our needs and to share. Seeing all the bottles of syrup lined up on the counter feels like a really good start to the spring. The snow is going, but the trees have not shown any green yet.

Everyone was hurrying to finish as many of the winter projects as possible and get the summer ones started before mud and mosquitoes hit. Our blankets and clothing are finally all dry enough to take indoors.

Elaine is proud of her teeth and shows them to everyone. She is walking herself around by hanging onto things and getting very fast at getting where she isn't supposed to be. In other words, a typical baby.

We have hens getting broody, new kid goats and another caribou. We are going to either have to expand or trade off some of our stock.

One of the kid goats died shortly after birth, so we are attempting to make

homemade rennet for the cheese making. We
cleaned the stomachs, they have several, and
opened and dried them. Then cut into very
small pieces. In theory, it should work. We
may have cleaned them too well to have it
work right. Trial and error shows us what
will work and what doesn't. However, the
way things are now, we can't afford much
error.

Chapter 23

Thad and Kara seemed to have an understanding of some sort and get along very well indeed.

Roman and Rose may or may not have. They enjoy working together and spend a lot of time together, but both also enjoy their own company.

Kara's adult children each have someone in their lives, but have not totally decided on what they want in the future.   Her grandchildren are a joy to everyone there.

Jeremy and Ashley are doing well in their marriage.   They would like to have children, but so far are not putting that as a priority.

Will and Shari are enjoying their twins so much and doing very well in their marriage. He is everything her first husband was not. A truly loving husband and partner.

Dan and Melanie will soon have their child. They have some problems, each is so used to being on their own, they don't think about the other person first. They are both trying to do better and now are focusing on the child and trying to put its welfare ahead of what they want to do. Their marriage is indeed a work in progress.

Al and Natalie now have a fine little boy. He was born a couple of days ago. Farren is becoming a happy young man and adores Natalie and the baby and thinks Al knows everything worth knowing. He is learning how to be a good hunter and trapper while not over harvesting the area he uses.

We are all doing pretty good and are looking forward to summer.

Some of the recipes mentioned in this book are given below.   More can be found in my cookbook, "Don't Use A Chainsaw In The Kitchen."

BASIC DRY CURE

Mix these dry ingredients together,
4 pounds Brown Sugar
2 pounds plain or pickling salt, not iodized
 ½ pound black pepper
 Sprinkle a thin layer in the bottom of a stainless steel or glass pan. Rub some all over the meat and sprinkle another layer over the meat when it is placed in the pan.   Sprinkle a layer over the whole pan of meat and place in a cool area.   The next day, rearrange the meat and rub more cure into the meat, repeating layers of cure and layers of meat.   Then do this every day until a slice into the meat shows uniform   color to the center of the meat or

to the bone.   Shake well and hang to dry
before smoking a few days to add flavor and
preserve the meat.

You may store this mix in a glass jar.
This is the best cure for jerky that I've ever
tried.   I also use it for ham, bacon and
shoulders being cured.   I do not like to use
saltpeter, and all it does is retain the red color
of the meat.
Variation: Red pepper flakes or cayenne for a
spicy cure.   Black pepper for flavor on bacon.

CHICKEN FRIED MOOSE STEAK

Pound thin or cube boneless moose steak.
Dip in seasoned flour (garlic & season salt)
Dip in water, milk or cream
Dip in bread crumbs or cracker crumbs
Let set for about 5 minutes while you heat oil
for frying in a heavy skillet.   Brown on one
side, turn and brown on the other side.   Serve
with cream gravy if you want to.

OLD FASHIONED MINCEMEAT

2 pounds lean meat, cooked and coarse ground

½ pound suet, ground fine

5 pounds tart apples, cored, peeled, chopped fine

2 pounds raisins

1 pound currants

4 cups fruit juice

1 ½ cups water or broth

3 cups brown sugar

3 t. salt

2 t. allspice

2 t. cinnamon

3 t. nutmeg

2 t. cloves

1 t. mace

Mix all together in large kettle. Boil for 20 minutes, stirring often to prevent scorching. Either pack in crock and float brandy on top or:

Pack into clean hot jars, add 1T. Brandy on top and put on lid and process at 10 pounds pressure for 90 minutes or:

Make several pies, adding 1 T. brandy over each filled pie before adding top crust. Bake until nicely browned, serve warm.

AMERICAN MOZZARELLA

INGREDIENTS:
1 gallon milk
1¼ teaspoon citric acid powder (from local pharmacy) dissolved in ½ cup cool water
½ tablet Junket Rennet (from local supermarket) suspended in ¼ cup cool water
Dissolve 1¼ tsp. citric acid powder into ½ cup cool water. Add to milk and stir well. Heat milk to 31C (88F) over boiling water in a small skillet. Dissolve ½ tablet Junket Rennet into ¼ cup cool water. Stir thoroughly into warmed milk mixture. Let set undisturbed for 1-2 hours, until a clean break is achieved. Cut curd into ½ inches cubes. Over low heat, stir the curds and whey gently to keep the curds separated and temperature uniform until temperature reaches 42C (108F). Hold at 42C (108F) for 35 minutes, stirring every five minutes to keep curds separated and off the hot bottom. Collect curds by pouring curds and whey through a fine cloth held in an 8 inch sieve over same covered container, let drain for 15 minutes. Save whey to make ricotta (You bring the acidified whey to 95C, cool, filter particulates). Break up curd, thoroughly mix in 1 teaspoon salt. Place 1 cup salted curd into 2 cup measure. Microwave on

high (1000 watts) for 45 seconds (adjust the time so that you get the desired elasticity). Try using a warm oven and testing every few minutes. Separate hot curd from container with the back of a fork, knead with hands to distribute heat evenly. Stretch and fold to make smooth and elastic, shape into a soft ball, pinch, place in refrigerator to solidify.

PLUM PUDDING

Combine 2 cups cooked ground meat, 1 cup sugar, 1 cup raisins, 1 cup chopped suet, 1 cup currants, 1 cup bread or cracker crumbs, 1/2 cup chopped candied orange peel, 1½ cup candied cherries, 1/2 cup candied pineapple and 1 1/2 cup candied fruit, 1 cup chopped apples, 3 eggs, 1/2 cup milk. Add 1 t. allspice, 1t. cinnamon, 1 t. soda and 2 cups flour. Pack in clean wide mouth pint jars to within 2 inches of top. Put lids on firmly, process in Pressure canner 60 minutes at 10 pounds pressure.

POP TARTS

3/4 C . shortening
3/4 C sugar
3 eggs
3 3/4 C flour
3 Tbsp baking powder
1/2 C preserves
1 egg yolk, beaten with 2 tbsp. light cream

Cream shortening and sugar. beat in one egg
at a time. Sift together flour and
baking powder, stir into shortening mix to
make a soft dough. Chill for 1 hour.

Turn dough onto a floured surface and roll
out 12 rectangles each 8 x 12".
Spread about a Tbsp of preserves over 1/2 of
each rectangle staying well within
the edges. Fold dough over the preserves and
trim the edges or crimp to close.

Place tarts on a greased cookie sheet and
brush w/the egg yolk cream mix. Bake
in a 350 degree F. oven for 20 minutes.

WALNUT SNOWBALLS

Ingredients
1 cup all-purpose or cake flour

1 1/2 cups walnuts, finely chopped
2-3 Tbsp sugar
1 teaspoon vanilla extract
1/4 pound butter (at room temperature)
Pinch of salt
Powdered sugar, to coat (about 1 cup)

Preheat the oven to 300°F and prepare a large cookie sheet. Do not grease.

Mix all the dry ingredients (flour, walnuts, salt, sugar) in a large bowl. Add the vanilla extract. Add the butter in little pieces, and combine everything together with your (clean!) hands until the mixture looks like a coarse meal with nut bits in it. Form the dough into small balls no larger than a walnut and place on the cookie sheet, spaced at least an inch apart from each other.

Bake for 35 minutes. When they are still warm, but cool enough to touch, roll the cookies in some powdered sugar. May need to roll again after they cool.

LINGONBERRY LIQUEUR (Low-Bush Cranberries) or BUSH MEDICINE
Very good for sore throats, coughs, flu symptoms, if made with Lingonberries, only.

First day: Crush 3 pounds Lingonberries, let stand 24 hours.

Second day: Add a Fifth of 190 proof grain alcohol, cover, let stand 24 hours. Boil 6 cups sugar with 3 cups water For 5 minutes, cool or refrigerate.

Third day: Strain juice (I use a colander and press mixture against the sides with a wooden spoon, the pulp doesn't hurt the liqueur, just shake before serving). Add syrup, stir well and bottle. Should age at least 3 weeks, but can be used immediately.

Variations:

Use 12 cups blueberries, blackberries, strawberries or raspberries instead of the lingonberries.

3 pounds of crushed peaches, apricots or other fruit, works quite well, only add the alcohol immediately after crushing.

May use vodka instead of grain alcohol, but liqueur will be very mild.

SUGAR BEET SUGAR

Instructions

Things You'll Need:

• A pound or more of sugar beets
• A large pan
• Colander

1. Wash and scrub the beets to remove any dirt or residue.
2. Chop small or shred the beets.
3. Place the beets into a large pot and add

enough water to keep them from sticking. Cook until the beets are soft and are losing their color.

4. Strain the beets, reserving the juice. Freeze the cooked beets for Borscht, cakes or dispose of, if desired.

5. Put the juice back on the stove and let it simmer until it reaches a thick, syrupy consistency. Stir constantly. The syrup should be similar in thickness to honey or corn syrup.

6. Remove from heat and let cool. As the syrup cools it will begin to crystallize. Cover with a dish towel or cheesecloth and let sit overnight.

7. Remove the crystallized beet sugar from the pan. Pound or otherwise break into small sugar crystals.

8. Use as you would store-bought sugar. Store as you would any sugar.

Tips & Warnings

• Beet sugar will not be pure white like store-bought sugar. It will still have a tinge of color.

• Beet sugar is better for you nutritionally than refined white sugar.

GREEN TOMATO JAM

Ingredients:

2 cups of green tomatoes, ground or grated

2 cups sugar

1 (3 oz) package of any flavor Jell-O

Directions:

1. Grind or grate tomatoes
2. Mix tomatoes and sugar
3. Bring to a boil
4. Boil 15 minutes
5. Remove from heat
6. Add Jell-O and stir well
7. Pour into jars and water bath 10 minutes
8. Enjoy!

PICKLED EGGS

- 12 hard-boiled eggs, peeled
- 1 large empty sterilized glass jar
- 4 cups vinegar
- 1 teaspoon salt
- 2 medium onions, chopped
- 1/3 cup sugar
- 1 tablespoon pickling spices   Optional: Add 1 cup beet juice for pink pickled eggs

Directions:
1 Put the peeled hardboiled eggs in the large jar.
2 Boil the remaining ingredients together for 5 minutes.
3 Pour over the eggs in the jar.
4 Cover; leave on counter overnight.
5 Keeps in refrigerator for weeks, in theory.
6 In reality, if you love pickled eggs, these

will disappear.

Other books by Rosalyn Stowell

The Beginning
An Alaskan PAW Novel
Written by Mrs. Rosalyn E. Stowell

This is a stand alone Book 1 in a Trilogy. It is situated in Alaska and written by someone that actually lives in Alaska and knows the climate and differences.
226 pages
ISBN/EAN13:
0615752470 / 9780615752471   ISBN-13: 978-0615752471 (Custom Universal)
ISBN-10: 0615752470
BISAC: Fiction / Romance / Suspense

The Dawn
An Alaskan PAW Novel
Written by Mrs. Rosalyn E. Stowell
This is stand alone book 3 in a Trilogy
Black & White on White paper
216 pages
R. E.\Stowell
ISBN-13: 978-0615769370 (Custom Universal)
ISBN-10: 0615769373
BISAC: Fiction / Action & Adventure

ALASKAN GOLD
Once Upon A Time In The North
An Alaskan Novel
Written By Rosalyn Stowell
A spur of the moment decision to check out her

inheritance in person just might be the best thing to ever happen or maybe not. Why won't ex-fiancés stay ex'd and how do you tell Toads from the Prince's? An ex Fiance' that refuses to admit he is an ex, an Attorney that is not looking for long term, an Environmentalist looking to shut down mining and the boy next door. How to choose?. Set in Alaska, maybe 20 years ago or so, join Jo as she learns about living and loving in the Bush and mining, not always in that order

About the writer:

I live 40 miles beyond phone or power lines. Over 50 miles beyond mail delivery. No TV, no radio, no door to door salesmen or politicians. Also no running water. It makes life simpler and a lot more fun. Of course, there is also no trash pickup or sidewalks. However, what there is, is a life full of interesting things to do and I have never been bored, ever.

I have lived in Alaska since 1969. I am a widow. I've operated heavy equipment, cooked, been a goldsmith, a taxidermist and a Registered Guide. I've built cabins and houses, waited tables, (very briefly, something to do with a pitcher of ice water and a customer) and peeled logs, painted pictures and worked as an artist's model to buy food and clothes for my children. I've even chauffeured for a while. I have held licenses as Boiler Operator, Taxidermist, Mill Operator, Registered Hunting Guide, Fishing Guide and for Mining. Life is interesting so be prepared for anything. You never know what is going to happen next.

My cookbook. Over 30 years in the making.

8.5" x 11" (21.59 x 27.94 cm)

Black & White on White paper
260 pages
R.E.Stowell
ISBN-13: 978-0615724324 (Custom Universal)
ISBN-10: 0615724329
BISAC: Cooking / Methods / Canning & Preserving
Over 400 recipes and assorted how-to
directions, on butchering, making sausage,
building a trappers cabin, tanning hides and
my autobiography at the back of the book.

Don't
Use
A
Chainsaw
In The Kitchen!!

Cabin Etiquette or Harmony in the Bush

1. Always go outside to cut frozen meat, if you are using a chainsaw.

2. If you open it, close it.

3. If you break it, admit it.

4. If you can't fix it, find someone who can, or replace it.

5. If it wasn't given to you or you didn't buy or make it, it's not yours, leave it alone.

6. Always leave some firewood for the next person.

7. If you make a mess, clean it up.

8. If you're sorry, say so.

9. If you kill something, clean it.

10. Leave everything in better condition than you found it.

11. If you value it, take care of it.

12. If you turn it on, turn it off.

13. If you borrow it, return it.

14. If you move it, put it back.

15. If it belongs to someone else, get permission to use it.

Rosalyn Stowell